Onwards! An Anthology

Onwards et al.

Published by Cooper D Barham, 2024.

This is a work of fiction. Similarities to real people, places, or events are entirely coincidental.

ONWARDS! AN ANTHOLOGY

First edition. June 25, 2024.

ISBN: 979-8224047499

Written by Onwards et al..

Foreword

In 2021, the city of Austin was only just beginning to shake off the dust following the pandemic. At long last, places were opening once more, and I was eager to find a new, in-person writing group, as writing can be a pretty lonely hobby at the best of times, but especially when you've been given no choice for a couple of years. Unfortunately, as a consequence, most local writing options had migrated to an exclusively online presence, or were too far away to be practical. After trying out the couple that were somewhat feasible, but not ideal, I decided to catapult myself beyond the veil of my comfort zone. Believing I couldn't be alone in my desire for creative community, I created the Onwards writing group.

The more I reflect on it, the more I recognize this to be one of the most significant, life-altering moves I've ever made.

It is difficult to distill the essence of the Onwards community into something as reductive as this simple foreword. Within them, there's a robustness, a depth, and a quality rarely found elsewhere. Time after time, I'm impressed by their inventiveness, diligence, vulnerability, adaptability. From a crowded coffee shop to a loud brewery, to our current home base of Dragon's Lair Comics & Fantasy, we've grown, changed, and steadily amassed what sometimes feels like a legion of strange and excellent people.

Through this community, I've found a wonderful partner, a wealth of incredible friends, and some of the best memories I'm likely to ever make. I'm deeply thankful for who they are, and proud of the camaraderie they've cultivated amongst one another. While I may have brought them together, they made the group their own. It's been an honor to witness.

As for this anthology, the convention is to say "I never imagined something like this happening," except in this case, that wouldn't be true. Considering the people involved, I couldn't help but believe in the potential. Sure, the process could have been more streamlined, and there was much to learn along the way. These things cannot be helped. What we've gained will be utilized to improve on future endeavors (a second anthology, while not promised, is already in discussion—this time with a theme, haha). Even so, there's an undeniable heart within these pages. The experimentation and freedom to dare greatly, and create something we could hold in our hands.

What I'm trying to say is, I'm glad we all have shared and continue to share in this journey together, even now. It is one of the most joyful and rewarding experiences of my life. You all deserve to be proud of what you've made.

Let's continue to explore new worlds and stories, pursuing the next horizon calmly, bravely, and without fail.

Thank you for reading.

Onwards!

Cooper

A Fine Meal

By Luis Alamo-Rivera

Content warnings: Disturbing imagery, death

From the rooftop of his hideout, far above the streets, Finn looked out over the slums of Elsed and could not help but smile. It was a practical smile, one directed not at the towering pyre in the lower city's square, nor at the fear and panic that had left the district's inhabitants—at least, those unable to flee—cowering in their homes, but at the opportunities they wrought: abandoned homes, empty rooftops, shuttered windows, and few, if any, keeping watch. All the things a thief could ask for. Satisfied, Finn turned from the grim vista and peered down at the reason he stood so close to the heart of his city's newest crisis.

To any casual observer, Rodrick's Knoll would have appeared as unremarkable an estate as the decrepit tenements that pressed in around it: the grass within its walled bounds was yellow and weedy, and the sparse hedge sculptures that adorned its lawn were in desperate need of pruning. The chateau at the lawn's center, a three-storied gray block of a building with narrow windows and juttings eaves, also lacked all semblance of grandeur, instead looking more like a prison in the dusky gloom. Like a barnacle-crusted oyster, however, its humble exterior held a precious secret. Not gold nor jewels, though there were surely plenty of those present, but a more valuable treasure: spice.

And this particular spice was the crown of the Emperor's own kitchen, the single most valuable commodity His nation had to offer, and Finn's meal ticket out of squalor. He'd never had it himself—scant few outside the nobility had ever seen the stuff, let alone tasted it—but he had heard it described once by his father, the words like brands in his memory. "The taste of a dessert," he'd said. "Warm and sweet and dry, hearth fire incarnate." Wars had been fought for its access, kings' ransoms paid for a single stone of the stuff. And below, within that brick of a building, was a whole cup.

Finn's mouth watered at the thought—how would it taste, he wondered. Would it match the measure of his imaginings? Could it ever? All that had stood between him and that answer was the Knoll. That, and the guards stationed inside.

There were a dozen of them, according to the Fence, all well-armored, well-armed, experienced, two of their numbers actual redjackets. Even so, Finn had practically jumped out of his hammock the moment the old miser had read the take aloud to the Keep's denizens, snatching the contract from his wrinkled hands so fast, he had nearly ripped the document clean in half.

"That one's a real piece of work, even for you," the Fence had said from between pulls of his pipe. "No one's made it past the lawn yet."

"Well, then," Finn replied, not bothering to look up, transfixed by the detailed layout of the manor, the manpower, the take. Especially the take. "I'll just have to be more careful."

He'd set about casing the place that same day, spending countless subsequent hours tallying the guards, noting their habits, and mapping various points of entry and egress, with a rare enthusiasm he hadn't felt in years. At first it seemed a simple enough job, the risk well worth the prize...but the more he learned of the obstacles before him, the truer the Fence's warning became.

Firstly, there were the walls circling the estate: two stories of washed, featureless stone topped with jutting overhangs and parapets to rival the duke's own palace. A simple enough hindrance to overcome, crowded as it was with buildings pressing in on all sides. The real problem came from the sentries patrolling their tops; a pair of ex-redjackets, their status clear by the cross-barred medals on their lapels. They scanned the streets below with bloodshot eyes, their hands more often occupied with mugs of ale than their rifles or torches. Sauced as they were though, Finn could count on one hand how many times he'd seen either of them neglect their patrol for more than a few minutes.

Of the guards within the manor itself, there were not a dozen, as the Fence had claimed, but *twenty*: ten stationed within the manor at all times, their shifts never deviating. All in all, as the Fence had foretold, the entire thing seemed a wash.

Then came news of the sickness in the lower city and the cordon soon after.

An unprecedented danger to the whole of Elsed, as the Magistrate had put it, a lethal malady not to be taken lightly, though they refused to give it so much as a name.

To Finn, the excitement around the news sounded no different than the panic that had surrounded the black tongue flare-up in the upper ward and the scarlet fever scare before that, both swiftly dealt with and forgotten about. Still, there was an air of anxiety to this latest sickness, one made all the more potent by the tight lips around the details. All anyone knew of it were vague mentions of scurvy-like symptoms and some kind of mysterious mania to those afflicted.

Finn was sure the ministry would handle it the way they had all its contemporaries, given enough time, but for the poorer merchants and the aristocrats in the area, who often bucked at the first sign of peril, it proved more than enough reason to flee. The current manor lord, a merchant whose name Finn couldn't rightly remember, was no exception, making off in the dead of night with only the clothes on his back, a dozen or so suitcases, and just as many personal guards. That left a threadbare crew of five for the chateau and its grounds, a number Finn was confident he could handle.

Yellow torchlight suddenly flickered below his perch, forcing the thief to duck his head. Peering over the ledge, he watched as a ragged crew of green-and-black-clad city guards led by two redjackets stomped down the avenue below. They waved their electric lanterns about the empty streets in wide, frantic arcs, the militaristic redjackets leading them with barking commands at every turn. None cared to look up, their heads hung low, fatigued from the long hours or else intent on the hunt for wayward citizens defying the curfew. Either way, the sight of their misery put another, more genuine, smile on the thief's face, one that stayed there long after the retinue had gone.

Only when Finn stood and considered the gap between his perch and the Knoll's wall did his good humor falter. While the wall itself rose to an even height with his side of the rooftop, the distance between them was daunting, no two ways about it: nearly ten feet end to end, with the landing a mere sliver of space between the parapet's merlons. Of all the dangers facing him that night, the jump that would get him there would be the most harrowing. One wrong step, and he would either break his legs on the cobblestone below or split his head open on the walls, themselves. The thief stood there for a while, imagining himself taking that leap, hoping for some last-minute stroke of genius that would illuminate any other way forward. But none came.

He bit his lip, then turned and walked to the other end of the roof, counting his steps for what had to be the dozenth time that night as he did so. Still fifteen paces, no matter how badly he wished there were more.

He looked at his bare hands, held them tight against his chest to keep them from shaking. *They'll say I'm losing my touch*, he mused, sure that his brothers at the Keep would have flown the gap without a second thought, just to prove his cowardice. But they were young, eager—two things Finn was long past.

He laid out his tools and inspected each item, more to distract himself from the madness of what he was doing than to take any real stock, and paused. He frowned, checked under and within the bag, pushing his various tools aside, but of his blade there was no sign. He swore and cast an eye at the fire escape leading down into the alley below, remembering he had used the missing stiletto for his supper earlier that evening.

He grunted in annoyance and made to climb down the iron-wrought stairs, but stopped short. Far below, two figures approached, torches in hand, the glare of the pale light hiding their features.

"I swear I saw someone up there," said one, a younger voice.

"You best hope to God you did, otherwise the corporal'll have your hide for wasting his time," said the other, an older man.

"It'll be worse if one of them sick slips the cordon. Then it'll be on *all* our heads. You heard the Manteia. What's the harm in checking?"

"My back, that's what's harmed."

"Ah come off it, you old codger," the younger said. "It'll be quick."

The clicking of steps followed, accentuated by the shaking creak of the fire escape leadened by their weight.

Shit, shit, shit. Finn bolted up and away from the stairs and looked around for anything that would serve as cover, but there was nowhere to hide, nowhere to escape to. His eyes snapped from the manor wall to the parapet, and the space between them. One place to escape to. He grimaced. *No more pussyfooting about it, then.*

"And if there is someone skulking about?" Said the older voice, noticeably out of breath. "Not like we can do much about it, garrison full as it is with them sick."

"Then we'll take a finger or two and send them on their way," the younger voice said with a casualness that sent a chill down Finn's spine. They were on the second story now, less than a minute from breaching.

"Make it quick, then," the older man grunted. "And remember not to look 'em in the eye, whoever it may be."

"I'll remember."

Time to go. Finn ran to the end opposite the edge, breath already short and ragged, and snatched up his satchel, the various tools jostling within. He checked his shoes, cinched the bag tight across his torso, gaze cutting to the landing all the while. The white glare of lamplight was growing, reflecting off of the escape's metal like motes of hellfire in moonlight. With one last deep breath, Finn took up a runner's position, gaze fixed on the ledge and the empty air beyond it, and took flight.

Gravel sprayed behind him as he ran, the cityscape and the stars wheeling above, blurring with his speed. Ten paces, five. The edge came on fast and hard. *It's not enough!* There was the briefest flash of panic as he neared it, his pace slowing ever so slightly, before his feet kicked off the ground and he was flying over the gap.

The moment Finn was in the air, he knew he wouldn't make it clean; the angle was wrong, the missed step possibly fatal, but there was no time to change course. All he could do was let out a subdued cry before his stomach slammed against the edge of the gap, the impact knocking the air from his lungs. Rough stone scraped against his arms and hands as he slid backwards, his fingers desperately clawing for purchase. At the last, he flung his arms wide and caught the side of the merlons to either side of him.

"See, there's no one here," the older voice said, now just behind.

"Hold on."

Finn's back prickled, a cold dread rising in him keener than the worst pain, and he kicked against the rough stone, trying his best to keep from grunting as he hauled himself up. He slid over, dropped a foot or so to the battlement's floor, then pressed himself low, peeking out from between the parapet's stone teeth.

Across the gap, the two watchmen wandered, fanning their torches about in fruitless search.

"What I tell you," the older voice said.

"I swear I saw someone looking at us over the edge there..."

One of the torches swung around and drew close and Finn ducked, pressing his back tight to the wall. Something clinked by his foot, and he looked down, amazed. Surrounding him nearly on all sides was a field of ale bottles. Empty, half filled, standing, shattered, they covered the parapet's floor like a forest of glass trees, broken only by a single wooden chair to his right. It was a miracle he had avoided crashing into them.

"You saw shit all," Finn heard the older man say. "Come on, we don't want to keep that redtop waiting."

A long silence. "Mhmp. Right."

And then, blessedly, the fire receded, the voice of irritated conversation fading to a murmur. It was nearly ten minutes before Finn dared to rise, wincing as he did so. Everything hurt. His arms stung, his chest felt like it had been caved in with a sledgehammer, but he grinned to himself all the same. The moment of highest doubt had passed: he'd made it.

Spirits lifted, he turned, picked his way through the glass minefield, and looked out across the half-acre of manicured lawn between himself and the manor. The space was well lit but here and there, eddies of shadows pooled between hedges and the sparse statues scattered throughout. There were no guards, as far as he could tell, and the whole of the residence, at least the side facing him, was dark and shuttered.

Assured, the thief wedged his hooked rope between the bricklayers and began his descent down the far side of the wall. He went slowly, trying his best not to think of what would happen if the masonry broke or the rope frayed, expecting at any moment to hear an alarmed shout come from behind him, or to feel the prick of a slug tearing into his shoulder. Fortunately none came, and he landed on the soft grass without incident. Crouching, not wasting a single second, the thief crossed the lawn in a brisk sprint, darting from one pocket of dark safety to another, the manor rearing closer before him.

While the old fortress had looked almost ageless from afar, as Finn approached, he saw that its stone was indeed weathered from decades of blowing winds and pockmarked from grievous assaults from years long past. Finn wondered, and not for the first time, what had compelled a man of Rodrick's status to choose such a bleak, brutally practical edifice as his home. The man was middling, sure, but not without means.

Someone with more than a few bolts of precious silk and spice to keep safe? Finn thought. Though what, he could hardly guess; the list of contraband was long indeed under the new duke. Whatever the reason, Finn would find out soon enough.

He eyed the manor's eave, measuring the distance with thumb and forefinger. He didn't like the look of the hairline cracks running throughout much of the stonework, but the masonry appeared solid, with not a loose stone anywhere in sight. It would have to do.

He fished out another bundle of rope from his pack and let it sail in a long arc over the manor's eave, the steel hook affixed to its end finding purchase after a long second of dragging. He gave it a fierce tug, and when he was sure it would hold, began to climb. Slowly he went, every inch a labor, but his arms were strong from countless past climbs, and before long, he was mere feet from the roof.

Then, he heard it: a snap like twigs breaking, and then a creak as the window right below his heels creeped open. The thief went still, scarcely daring to draw breath, waiting for the face of a curious guard or the barrel of a rifle to come swinging in his direction. Seconds ticked by, and then minutes. Seven passed before Finn's burning arms could take no more and he was forced to keep climbing. He reached upward... And then nearly screamed when the rope suddenly slackened and he dropped.

For a breathless moment, his mind turned blank, consumed with pure panic, before the hook caught again and he bounced in place, nearly losing his grip. He looked up, eyes wild, and was greeted with a shower of dust and loose rocks, the larger stones bouncing off his forehead. Half blind and coughing, he scrambled for the sill of the open window, his already raw hands slapping against its coarse frame. An instant later, there was a crumbling thud, and Finn once again dropped, managing this time to catch himself on the sill. He watched in dismay as the rope passed by him in a snaking flail, the iron hook at its end racing it to the bottom.

The thief spat and braced himself against the frame, the panic fading, his mind already turning the next possible options over. He couldn't get down: there were no handholds, not even a divet to dig his toes into, and he couldn't climb up for much the same reason. The plan had been to sneak in through the attic, where he would have an escape should he be caught and forced to retreat. That was scrapped. The only way forward now was the shadowy entrance before him. He tried to get a better look at the room's interior, but no matter how he turned his head, he could see nothing but a small patch of its ceiling. His arms were burning now, his strength failing. There was no more time.

With a trembling sigh and with his heart in his throat, Finn pulled himself up and entered the manor.

The stench of soil and strong alcohol hit Finn like a slap to the face, the suffocating stink made all the more potent by the darkness within the unlit room. Enough light spilled in from outside, however, that Finn could make out that, but for a cot pushed up against the far wall, the room was empty.

Lying on that bed was a man—a man wearing forest green trousers and black leather boots, with the glint of a medal on his lapel, its cross-barred shape clear despite the gloom. Not any old soldier then, but one of those two redjackets the thief had figured long gone. Finn tensed, readying to bolt, but the figure only continued to lie inert as though sleeping. There was something unusual in the figure's posture, though: his back was slightly arched, arms to the side, his fingers splayed as though reaching for something. Most of his face was obscured by a thick rag, but black hair spilled out over the pillow, itself stained with dried sweat.

As Finn's eyes adjusted to the dimness, he saw the cause of the man's contortions: thick, white bands criss-crossed the length of his torso in a blanket that would have held an elephant still. Rags were piled at the bedside and someone had hung a five-pointed star above the cot's headboard, words of prayer written on each spoke. A token of grief for the dying. And the sick.

Finn swore, threw a hand over his mouth, and backed away. Had he touched anything on the way in? No, no, he'd barely stepped inside before he'd found the corpse, and someone had taken pains to keep the space clean, the only bodily stains tight around the bed. Producing a handkerchief from his pocket, he sniffed the air through it, noting the lack of foul vapors. An assuring detail, though not an infallible one; black tongue was notorious for spreading through a whole community without a single breath shared between its victims, and red fever sprouted anywhere it pleased, including the royal quarters, with impunity. Who knew what this new ailment was capable of?

All the more reason to get out of there. Finn neared the door, inspecting the hinges for patches of rust that could screech out his presence, dousing them silent with oil from his pack when he found them. He turned the knob. Locked—and from the outside. Little surprise, given the room's occupant. The lock itself fortunately proved to be of such antiquated design and so ill-kept that it practically sprang open at the thief's touch, light from the outer hall spilling in through the smallest crack.

He was just about to leave, when, after making one last habitual glance over his shoulder, something caught his eye. He paused at the door's threshold, squinting into the dark behind him. And spotted a glimmer.

He nudged the door further open, letting light from the hall stream into the room. Something glinted in the darkness, its source resting at the dead guard's side. Finn knew that shine. He took a step back into the room, moving a little to one side to let more light in. Sure enough, the glimmer came from a gold pocket watch affixed to a steel chain wrapped around the dead man's right hand. A modest trinket, simple in design, yet it had to be worth at least half a hundred ducats...

The thief chewed the inside of his cheek and looked out past the door into the hall, but there was no real deliberation, not when the take was so easy. Holding his breath, he ambled back to the cot, and, kerchief in hand, expertly slipped the chain off the man's wrist. As he did so, his fingers grazed the guard's skin. It was warm—scalding, even—as though the man were not dead, but still suffering from the fever that had likely killed him.

Finn snatched his hand away, but the man did not move, still as stone. Although Finn was sure the guard would have bashed his head in without hesitation, were he alive and hale, he felt pity for the poor sod. It seemed a nasty way to go, straining and fighting to the very last. But the thief put it out of his mind, returning to what really mattered.

It was a fine piece, the watch: plain, but well made. On the back, "To my love" was engraved in fine lettering. Inside was a picture of a young woman, her features diminished somewhat by the wear of time, but managing to shine through all the same. The clock face was cracked, a knock against its value, to be sure, but the hands still moved as inexorably forward as the time it kept. Finn slipped it into his shirt pocket, took one last long look at the corpse, and moved on.

The hall beyond was almost as dim as the room preceding it, though far more ostentatious. Glass sconces lined the stone walls, the old bulbs within them dim and weak, and a long, green carpet stretched across its length, rendered almost black in the low light. Paintings of various dimensions hung, featuring bland landscapes and portraits of dour-looking noblemen thrown together with no sense of intent or cohesion. On either side, doors passed in regular intervals, most shut, a handful open, the unoccupied rooms beyond them in various states of neglect and despondency. At the end was a flight of stairs descending into still more dimness.

Finn stopped at the landing, peering down to the first floor, straining his hearing for footfalls or the lilting of voices and, upon hearing neither, descended.

Outwardly, his every movement was steady and measured, but inside, Finn's heart pounded like a maelstrom. Each step was a loaded risk, every groan and creak a damning accusation. And to think, once he had relished the thrill, thinking of theft and the breaking into of homes much like a game, one with rules, winners, and losers. Long years and too many maimed and dead comrades had cured him of that illusion.

The first floor fortunately held no obstacles and was, in fact, a near twin to the second—dimly lit, slightly musty, gaudily adorned—but for another hall stretching before him. At its end was a large, well-lit space. The foyer. The storage vault lay just past it, nestled at the end of a long corridor to the right of the central staircase next to the kitchen.

Only...where were the guards? Aside from the dead one upstairs, there was no sign of them. The thought didn't relax the thief. They could be anywhere, hiding in any one of the dozens of locked rooms, relaxing in the main hall, having themselves a late-night meal in the kitchen. Lying in wait just beyond the corner...

He shook the thought from his head. It was just as likely they were sleeping, turned in early for the night, lulled to complacency by the plague and its curfew, or, better yet, withered away in their own musty corner somewhere out of sight, dead and harmless. Finn didn't really believe either scenario; he'd never had that kind of luck, but it was enough to keep him moving.

The foyer, like the rest of the manor, was vacant. Unlike the rest of the estate, however, the space was properly grand, the tiled floor waxed and polished to a mirror shine, the wide oak banisters of the grand staircase at its center varnished and gleaming. Overhead, a gorgeous chandelier hung by silver chains, its myriad bulbs bright and undimmed, and along the walls were rich banners of green and black. Between them, a menagerie of felled animals stared out from oak mounts, toothy maws of various predators yawning in defiance.

Finn crossed the space, the dominating silence broken only by the scuffing of his padded boots, his back prickling all the way, exposed and easy to spot against the empty marble. The hall to the right of the staircase was quiet and dark, but a bright light shone from an unseen source further in, flickering like a beacon. He drew closer, flattening his back against the wall, his breath shallow. At the crux, he paused, fished out a curve glass from his pack, and held it to the corner, turning it slightly to just barely catch the light.

Shapes twisted and stretched in its reflection and then resolved into the figures of two guards at the hall's end, the silver and green of their uniform loud in contrast with the pale stone around them. Only, they were not standing, but instead were slumped against the door's frame, one resting their head against the wall to their right. Between them was the vault.

And it was open. A single lightbulb hung inside, illuminating the space within in sharp, glaring yellow light. Crates, stacked from floor to ceiling, lined the interior, and sacks of grain and miscellaneous items were strewn about the floor in disparate piles, as though dumped. And by the door...

Finn sucked in a breath, the glass nearly slipping from his hands. He looked about, expecting the flash of a blade or the head of a hammer to fill his vision, but there was no attacker coming for his head, no cry of alarm. He turned back a lump of fear in his throat.

He didn't need a second glance to know what he'd seen in the looking glass, but he took one, anyway. Blood: a pool of it by the threshold, accompanied by torn clothes and a dismembered arm, its hand reaching as if its owner had been hacked mid crawl. Finn's mind raced, gaze affixed to the butchery.

Had another crew caught wind of the take and beaten him to it? No, he would have heard of the affair at some point in the preceding months, and besides, the blood looked freshly spilled and he had not seen anyone attempt an entry before himself. That wasn't to say the feat was impossible. There could have been some entryway he'd overlooked, a hidden drain ditch or a path along the river bank.

The thief looked back over his shoulder at the front entrance. The voice of reason in the back of his head said he could leave, right then and there: rush out the front entrance and climb the wall and be grateful for having at least found the pocket watch to pawn. It was fine advice, sensible, but he turned back to the vault, the harsh light within almost beckoning. The vault was *open*, the guards (most of them, anyways) all accounted for and decidedly indisposed. In that light, it was easy to see the massacre as a golden opportunity, one he might never see again.

Of course, if he was wrong, and there was some further trap lying in wait for him, he might not survive the night, let alone the interminable time between. But he didn't think so. Why lay a trap, especially one so elaborate, for a nameless thief they'd had no clue was coming? With that in mind, the risk did not seem so great, and the rewards more than enough to make up for it. Finn grit his teeth and rounded the corner.

The two slumped guards stared at some invisible horizon as he approached, their swords sheathed. They'd been caught by surprise, then, Finn guessed. He raised the kerchief over his nose again to block out the stench of copper and emptied bowels, and moved closer, tense as a sprung coil and ready to bolt at the slightest provocation.

Inside the strong-room, a third guard—the owner of the missing limb Finn had spotted—was lying face down on the linoleum. Unlike the two outside, his saber was drawn and coated in red. Around the corpse were piles of coins spilled from bags, broken busts of Kaenic emperors, plates of silver, and shattered porcelain. Some of the shelves were bare, and one entire pallet was tilted on its side, its myriad contents (mostly rolled parchments and writs of receipts gobbed with wax) scattered.

Two guards dead, two nowhere in sight, gold and wealth missing in the wake of violence... Finn was no academic, but he could put two and two together: he hadn't been the only one to see that night and the chaos for the opportunity it was.

Despite the blood and the stench of death, Finn was relieved, the weight of fear and anticipation lifted off his shoulders. So, no third party to account for, no laid trap, just a banal tale of greed and betrayal that had nothing to do with him. It was good news, but it was a brief reprieve, one smothered by the possibility that what *he* sought might have been part of the plunder.

He cast an eye across the room, pocketing what few worthwhile baubles he could find as he moved through it, barely registering their worth, his anxiety rising in pitch every time he drew open a burlap sack or a screwed canister and found only basic treasure inside. He brushed lesser jewels out of the way, letting them clatter to the ground, sifted through heavy stacks of gold bars and silver plates, tossed aside enough valuables to pay his debts with coin to spare, but of the spice, there was no sign.

And why would there be? Of all the treasures in store, it would have been the easiest to carry, and priceless, besides. He could hardly blame another thief for beating him to the mark—weeks of planning, wasted, his dreams crushed to fine powder. A petulant rage rose in his chest, his fingers itching to act.

He gave in to the impulse, smashing an expensive-looking vase, knowing all the while how pathetically he was behaving and not caring. None of it did anything to soften the bite of failure.

He slid to the ground, exhausted, and rested on his haunches, looking at the pilfered loot about him between splayed fingers. Any self-respecting thief would have counted himself lucky to have but a fraction of that haul, and yet all he tasted was bitter defeat.

He paused, smacked his lips, pursed them. That wasn't disappointment on his palette. He looked at his hands under the light. There was a thin layer of brown dust on his palm. Finn's heart skipped a beat. Not dust. He raised it to his mouth, sniffed.

Woody earth, a sting of spice akin to cloves, sweet and somehow...warm. The taste was much the same, a surprising punch of spiciness at the end that made him hoot in delight. It was the taste of a lit hearth, the kiss of sunshine on a chill winter afternoon—exactly as his father had described all those years ago.

He looked down at the vase he'd smashed. Its body had broken near the top, leaving a shallow bowl now tipped on its side. From its mouth, fine brown powder spilled onto the bare stone floor, the aroma which had previously been obscured by the stench of viscera obvious now, loud and beautiful.

Finn fell to his knees, rubbing the fine stuff between his fingers, recipes and the shape of dishes floating across his mind's eye like a veritable buffet of possibilities. The vague sweetness of it naturally brought up images of flaky crust, baked porridge, and pudding. And with that, visions of himself decked in fine white linen instead of the dingy leather that had become like a second skin for him, a line of hungry visitors out the door desperate to be served his fare. How would Finn's father see him then, were he alive? Would he be proud, knowing that his son had finally learned his lesson?

Grinning, lost in thought, Finn emptied a small pouch of its jeweled content, the precious stones clattering to the ground like spare change, before carefully depositing the brown powder into it with a silver spoon, discarding it when he had finished. He cinched it shut, held it in his palm, feeling the weight. Nearly a pound, he guessed. A pound! Three times what he had expected, more than he had ever hoped for. With a contented sigh, he carefully placed the pouch within his satchel and picked his way through the vault, stepping lightly over pools of blood and broken ceramics alike, a jaunty tune on the cusp of breaking out from his lips.

He stopped at the foyer's center and slowly turned in a circle, pausing to take in the space. It was grand, to be sure, but wasteful in Finn's eyes. His manor would be smaller, more compact, enough to fit a dozen rooms. What did anyone need with more? He glanced at the double doors of the kitchen, the light of faint lamps flickering through the porthole, then back at the manor's entrance and its fastened lock. The thief bit his bottom lip. *What's a few more minutes?*

He was rich with jewels and leadened bags of coin, and could soon afford a kitchen of his own and all the staff necessary to run it. But given how strict the new duke was on lowly crime, it might take months to fence what he needed for such an endeavor without drawing undue attention. There was the small kitchen back at the Keep, sure, but that was a paltry, mean thing built only for providing the barest necessities. He wanted to start practicing *now,* even if it was for a bunch of lowlifes and criminals.

A pang of excitement in his chest swelled and, despite the voice of caution keening in his ear, the rest of him pulled him toward the swinging doors and the promised land beyond.

The kitchen was everything Finn hoped it would be, and more. On either side of him, an array of neatly stacked pots and pans rested atop two long-range stoves, cloves of garlic and bushels of onions, parsley, lemons, and limes hanging from hooks from the ceiling above them for easy reach. Along the walls were shelves upon shelves of cookware and plates, a huge pot taking its place at the end of the room. Two iron doors with latches bordered the pot—the larder and pantry, he presumed. The air inside was smokey, and subtly tinted with the vestiges of a long-ago prepared meal. Mutton and gravy.

Finn traced a hand along one of the flat stove tops, thinking how the kitchen would have looked with a full complement of servants and sous chefs working the fires. A memory of his father, always stern and regal and powerful in Finn's mind, drifted up from the dredges of his past. Age and stress had already made its mark on his father's skin, lining it with wrinkles too soon for his age. He was standing at the kitchen's head, pointing, nodding, and shouting instructions to his staff as a conductor might his orchestra, his own hands busy in preparation. Together as one, they scrambled in circuits about the kitchen, their movements as smooth and choreographed as any play. They had the honor that night of cooking for the duke—a crowning moment for Finn's old man, maybe his proudest, looking back.

The thief, in his youth, hadn't cared, his thoughts ever turned to the gambling dens and the bets he had made there with ducats he hadn't earned. Why did he have to be there? He'd told his father before he had no interest doing women's work and he repeated it then with a wretched sullenness that fifteen years later still made him cringe with shame. Never would he forget his father's stricken face, the fury, the shame...

The duke had loved the meal, and lavished his anonymous servers with compliments, but by then, Finn's father's mood had soured and he accepted the accolade with little celebration. There was no later lecture at home, no heated argument over how Finn was wasting his future.

"There's no changing you," was all his father had said. "I see that now."

A bulb of regret clogged Finn's throat at the memory, still bitter and sharp after all those years. He sucked in a breath, subduing the feeling. It would be different now—*he* would be different.

Right after he scooped some first-class produce and cutlery. *Then* he would be done.

As he'd thought, every utensil was expertly forged, polished, and sharpened—each a precious tool and work of art in their own right. At least, compared to the rusted slivers of pig iron and pewter that passed for cutlery back at the Keep. He grabbed a particularly fine silver ladle, plucked rare limes from their hangings, and emptied vats of truffle oil into small glass containers, all of which he stuffed into his already ladened satchel.

When the weight of it all began stretching the seams, he began stuffing his pockets instead, a strange mania overtaking him, that shard of the thief within prodding Finn to take more and more. Normally, he considered himself above the compulsion, but he obliged it, just this once; after all, this was his last haul. Biting into an apple, Finn inspected the pot, sniffed at its empty interior, and slid a finger along its inside, tasting the residue. Venison, not mutton. Close enough.

The larder, lined with hanging carcases of butchered beef and pigs, held little he could take with him. The pantry, a treasure trove of its own, was bolted shut and padlocked. A triviality; the lock was a three-chambered tumbler, sturdy but hardly an obstacle for his deft fingers. Still, the fact that it was there at all was promising. He lifted the lock to inspect its mouth, and felt a patch of something flakey on its back. Blood. It coated the lock, the chain, a thin layer of it extending to the pantry handle in the shape of a smeared handprint. Old and coagulated, a day or two from turning to dust entirely.

Finn pursed his lips, wondering at how the kitchen staff of a lord could be so sloppy. Even the Keep's cooks—a generous term for the brutes—knew to wash themselves after a butchering.

Fetching a clean washrag, Finn set upon the lock, flicking away crusted blood that had congealed at the mouth of the tumbler, and made short work of it, nodding to himself as the hunk of metal clattered to the floor. The door was heavy wood studded with iron, but it swung open easily, the hinges silent.

Almost immediately, Finn was struck with a gust of hot, fetid air, a miasma of dampness and the intimate stench of unwashed bodies. And blood, now familiar. The sanded floor was covered in it, mixing with the sawdust in a garish red paste that caked the floor, making it both coarse and slippery. Foodstuffs lined the shelves closest to him: vibrant fruits and vegetables, rows of canned and pickled produce, wheels of various cheeses. The light inside had gone out, the only form of illumination coming from the kitchen lamp behind him. His shadow stretched into that dimness, reaching across the far shadows of the long pantry...and falling upon a crouched figure in the far corner.

The man's back was to the thief, the tips of his coat's lapels dragging along the ground, daubed red with the blood pooling there, but there was no mistaking the green coat. Thick white bands, frayed and torn, were piled behind him, twins to those that held the dead man just upstairs. The loose, fibrous strands soaked in the sanguine pool, turning them crimson.

The man's head was bent downward, bobbing slightly, elbows tucked in before him, the sounds of tearing flesh and teeth against bone drifting up like an echo from the depths of the Seventh Circle, itself. Before the figure lay the remains of a human shape. At least, Finn thought it was human. The legs terminated at the thigh, great disks of blood and gore marking where the flesh had been removed in neat, brutal cuts. Bones lay close to the man—thighs, foreleg, an arm—all stripped clean.

Finn stood there, dumb, uncomprehending, the apple falling from his open mouth. It hit the ground with a wet, cracking splat.

The figure ceased its motion, the sounds of feasting stopping all at once. Slowly, degree by degree, the head of the man turned as though in a dream, revealing an older, lightly stubbled face. Coated in blood. His teeth were bared, strips of red flesh hanging like shingles over his lips. A chunk of the man's cheek was missing, tongue visibly loling in his mouth. But of all the horrors, the worst were his eyes. They squinted against the light, but there was no mistaking their color: gold, shimmering in the dark like the eyes of a predator.

Small motes of light twinkled in the center of those golden rings, deep within the man's black pupils, dancing will-o-wisps against a night sky. They seized Finn's attention like a vice, as though demanding to be seen, to be understood, and though some distant part of him recoiled at their sight, he could not look away.

They stared at one another, Finn rooted to the spot, then the man blinked and the light was gone. The soldier shook himself like he was waking up, and he looked again at Finn with a wan, dreamy smile, one the thief would have found charming if not for all the gore.

"J?" the man said. "It's you, isn't it?"

He turned fully around to face Finn, revealing a small, gleaming medal pinned to the lapel of his coat: two stripes bisected with a diagonal red line...

Finn's body moved. He did not ask it to; he was still too surprised to form coherent thought, let alone formulate a semblance of a plan, but his instincts moved him all the same, drawing his hands forward and latching onto the edge of the heavy wooden door, hauling it with all his might. Within half a second, he had shut it, his hands working the chain and the lock. Too late.

He felt a dull impact, saw the world blur into a smear of motion, his body weightless in the air. There was a sudden thudding impact, a savage jolt of pain lancing through Finn's back, the sound of breaking glass and ceramics thundering in his ears.

He slowly sat up, bracing himself against a nearby cabinet, and watched in disbelief as the pantry door swung closed and then opened again. From the darkness stepped out the man, arms outstretched like a lector at his pulpit, that horrid smile still on his face.

"Quit the games," he said, the sound harsh and muddled by the torn cheek and lolling tongue. "I knew you would come, those faithless whoresons called you dead, but I knew better. I knew..." He followed this with a good-natured chuckle, but it stopped abruptly, the man's face going slack as his eyes finally fell on Finn.

"Who…who are you?" he said, his face contorting first with confusion before morphing into a grimace thick with suspicion, blood from the wound in his cheeks spurting obscenely onto his coat. "What have you done…with Jerran? Yes, Jerran…"

His eyes fell on Finn's satchel, at the smattering of treasure scattered about the floor, and then finally on the golden watch at the man's feet. Its clam had fallen open, revealing the now thoroughly shattered glass face and the picture of the woman within.

The man's gaze lost focus and he began to mutter to himself for a few seconds before bending over and retrieving the timepiece by its chain. He raised it to his vacant face.

"Misha…" he said, squeezing his eyes shut. Then, something seemed to click in the madman's mind and without warning or transition, the grimace of confusion became a furious scowl.

"A thief," he hissed, one fist closing about the locket, the other pointing a blood-stained finger at Finn, irises blazing like burnished bronze. "Just like those miserable robbers calling themselves 'comrades.'" Though the man's voice was barely above a hushed whisper and he had made no move, rage seemed to bleed out from him like a wave of physical heat.

"Now listen…" Finn said, struggling to his feet, "Wait…" He waved his hands before him, showing they were empty. Perhaps he could talk his way out of this, or at the least give himself time to think.

"Oh no, oh no, no," the thing said, baring its teeth. "No, I'll have your hands, thief. Both of them." It took a swaying, drunken step toward Finn, and then another before steadying itself on a length of stovetop. The metal beneath the guard's fist *bent*, screeching and tearing as though crushed by a vice.

The sound, deafening in the enclosed space, snapped Finn back to lucidity. Snatching up the satchel, he turned and shouldered through the kitchen's doors, running full sprint to the manor's front entrance, the animal heads on the walls leering at his terror. He slammed against the wooden door, hands pawing at the latch. He fumbled the bar, lifted it...

A screech, high and inhuman, pierced his ears—close! Too close! Without thinking, his body again acting on pure instinct, Finn pushed himself away from the door and dove to the ground. An instant later, there was a vicious crack from just over his shoulder. Splinters peppered his back, stinging, some slivers burying themselves into his flesh. The thief scrambled to his feet, throwing a glance over his shoulder as he sprinted toward the far hall.

The front entrance was a dented ruin, miraculously closed, but bowed in as though struck with a cannon, the metal trimming and delicate carvings that had adorned its surface a fractured memory. The madman was at its center, nestled in the crater he'd created like a sleeping infant. His eyes were open, gold irises staring hatefully at Finn. His arm was buried in the wood up to the shoulder, the sharp timbers snagging the man tight. Blood welled along the bicep, the flesh torn and flayed by splintered stakes.

"I'll find you, scum," he hissed, struggling against the wood and iron, the timber groaning its protest, unwilling to let him go.

The thing yelled something else out, but Finn was already sprinting full tilt to the vault, blood rushing in his ears, thoughts obliterated by the desperate need to escape. Despite his panic, he was cognizant enough to know that none of the manor's many rooms could protect him. Wood, as he'd just observed, was no safe barrier. Only the vault and its hundred pounds of iron could save him.

He rounded the corner, nearly slipped on the spilled blood of the slain guard at the strong-room's entrance, and dashed inside, hand snagging the door to slow his sprint. He twisted around and leaned against the heavy iron, sweat beading on his forehead from the effort.

A savage roar of triumph drifted in from the foyer, the sound of pounding feet short behind. The last thing Finn saw before the door finally slammed closed was the guard's furious scowl boring into him.

Where his left arm had been, there was now a gruesome stump of torn flesh and bone. Finn screamed, closed the door the last inch, and slammed the inner latch into place, backpedaling far enough to knock against the table that had held the spice vase.

The metal door thudded, the iron holding firm, sending dust and plaster falling like snow from the ceiling. The impact was largely muffled, remote, but Finn could imagine the terrible force working on the iron hinges and latch, the outer layer of the vault door denting with the impact.

Another thud, a dozen more after that, each more forceful than the last, accompanied with screams of fury that turned Finn's blood to ice. Shadows danced wildly, the bulb above Finn's head swinging with each impact. He imagined the thing getting hold of him, how easy it would be for it to break him like so much kindling—then pushed the thought from his head. He had to focus, had to figure a way out. But no matter where he looked, there was only the gray stone, surrounding him as a tomb might a corpse. Of course, there was also the hefty assortment of wealth. How ironic to be surrounded by such riches and have them mean not a damn thing.

Another impact, and a new, altogether more terrifying sound: the shaking of iron bolts coming loose.

Whatever that thing was, it was still a man, still vulnerable. Those terrible gaping wounds and the missing arm had made that clear. What pulpy mess, what contorted, tortured thing would come for him once that singular barrier keeping Finn alive reached its limit? He could scarcely imagine it, could only hope that the thing's body would give out before it came to that point. But the assault would not abate, instead rising in pitch and ferocity with every passing minute.

The thief searched his satchel, as though something within could save him. The hand crossbow that had lent him so much confidence seemed a paltry thing now, a child's toy fit only for amusement. Maybe he could blind the thing when it charged, but Finn had never been a good shot. Everything else seemed like useless trash, and the contents of the vault were little better, aside from a ceremonial hatchet that held no edge. He snatched it from its mount all the same. Better than nothing. Barely.

Another thud. Finn could see the iron door bending, the frame splintering, the concrete base cracking, as though it were a swinging battering ram on the other side and not a man. As impossible as it seemed, the man *would* get through. The only question was when.

How much more time would Finn have? Hours? Minutes? Some time at least, enough to curse the Fence for bringing him the job, in the first place, and himself for taking it. Mostly it was his own arrogance. In the end, he was no better than his foolish younger brothers, worse for having the experience to know better. The old man's word of warning about the potential deadliness of the job crossed his mind as though to rub the point in, and Finn winced thinking of his own flippant response: "Happens to us all eventually." Had he really said that?

Time crept on, the assault never ceasing, every thud like a stab to his heart. He paced the room as a starving rat would an empty cage, turning its contents over and over, hoping to find something, anything that could save him.

And then, something impossible happened. Beneath the earth, surrounded on all sides by stone and iron, Finn felt a cool breeze tickle the back of his neck—a slight gust, barely more than a hushed whisper, and perceptible only due to the sheen of sweat that layered his body.

He whirled, staring at the back wall: a slab of stone, bare but for a small table and a large, unadorned armoire pushed up against it. Finn closed his eyes, stretched his arms out before him, fingers searching for that sensation again. And he found it, just to his left where the wardrobe stood. He drew closer, wincing as the thing outside once more slammed itself onto the iron door.

Upon first inspection, the piece of furniture appeared to just be plain, unvarnished wood, its contents a smattering of expensive-looking Montic furs and little else of note. But something was off. The piece was old—much older than the rest of the furniture in the vault—and was weathered and splintered by time, if not the elements. Finn threw open the bifold doors, threw out robes and shirts and shoes, hundreds of ducats' worth of fashionable attire, onto the floor, leaving the wardrobe blank and bare. The back panel was a slab of undecorated wood. But running through its center, barely visible to the untrained eye, was a seam.

Finn could have danced and cheered, and if he was not so close to being mauled to death, he likely would have. Of course, he shouldn't have been surprised; the manor was a fortress built originally to withstand a siege. And what was a fortress without a route of escape? He tore at the panel, digging his fingernails into that seam, desperately searching for purchase and to his dismay not finding any. Likely there was some sort of hidden mechanism, a switch disguised as a cabinet knob, or an innocuous corner that would depress with some prodding.

"Sod this," he muttered, picking up the decorative hatchet in one hand and making short work of the flimsy wood, despite the hatchet's dullness. Behind the ruin of splinters was a small hatchway four feet long on all sides that angled down into inky blackness. A slight draft emanated from it, gentle as a caress.

There was no deliberation, no choice, really. Finn threw himself into the pit without a second glance.

The darkness was absolute, the press of the tunnel tight around Finn, the ladened satchel slowing his progress. Still, he managed, dragging himself forward and downward, all the while straining his ears for the sound of tearing metal and the growls of his pursuer. Eventually that, too, fell away, leaving only his own desperate exhalation, tight and animal in his ears.

Minutes passed, though whether it was five or ten, it was impossible to tell. He tried to ignore the weight of the stone surrounding him and the horrid notion that there would be no end to the tunnel, and focused instead on putting one hand in front of the other. The breeze grew stronger with every passing moment; there *had* to be an exit.

Sure enough, the darkness began to abate, his dirt-stained, bloody fingers reappearing once more from out of the inky blackness before him. Ahead—the distance hard to gauge—was a square of dim, orange light. Finn sucked in a breath, crawling all the faster, the light beckoning him on.

A loud bang echoed behind him. It was far away, muffled, but unmistakable. The thing had made it through. Dread gripped him, and Finn pushed himself forward, no longer crawling but clawing his way through the tunnel, his shirt riding up to his armpits, stomach and arms scraping against the rough-hewn stone. The square of light grew closer, inch by painfully slow inch, but the walls of the tunnel seemed to press in tighter around him, as though unwilling to let him go.

He was close, could taste the dusty must of soil and the bracing briny scent of the Korinthar. Suddenly, without warning, he came to a stop. His fingers pulled, his legs kicked, but his body refused to move. Caught. The thing had found him, sliding in the dark without a sound and now had Finn in its grip. The agony would come, the cracking of bone would fill his ears...

Only, he felt no claws, nor pressure on his ankle. The passage had indeed narrowed, and not just in his imagination.

He pulled himself forward with a growl, his legs kicking furiously, the scraping of loose rocks like nails against his ears. He twisted around, felt the pressure loosen, if only slightly, and then kicked off the inner wall, at last coming free to the tune of tearing cloth. A cacophonous tinkling filled the confined space, echoing maddingly about him, the cold touch of pilfered coins, jewels, and silverware skirting along his back and thigh, tracing dread along its path. The satchel had ripped, caught on a stray piece of masonry, spilling his future behind him. Finn swore, tried to reach behind himself to grab at the bag, but the tunnel was too narrow, his arms unable to bend behind him, and succeeded only in spilling more of his stolen riches.

He looked back to the tunnel exit, three or so meters away, and dragged himself to it. What else could he do? Pulling himself through, he slithered out into the blinding glow, sliding more than falling onto the sandy floor below.

The air smelled of sewage and was thick with humidity. As Finn's eyes adjusted to the sudden brightness, he could see that the light came from a series of bare bulbs hanging by strips of wiring from the rock ceiling. To his left was a channel of water, bordered by more jagged and glistening wet stone. Ahead, the channel extended some four meters before passing through a slimy, trash-choked sluice and into the Korinthar beyond.

Behind him, set into the rock, was the square mouth of the tunnel he'd just crawled through, a rusted grate on the ground beside it. Within it, was the treasure he'd dropped—barely more than an arm's reach away. He didn't need the voice of caution to tell him it was madness to go back for it.

But without the spice and its riches, what life did he have to look forward to? He could picture it with ease: one dangerous repetitious chapter after another, the difference between life and death decided by a store of luck he knew would not last, his sordid story ending one way or another with a lopped hand or a cut throat. He could change that, prove his father wrong, all he needed was that gold, that spice—a second chance.

He moved toward the yawning pit, steps shallow and hesitant, ignoring the part of him that screamed to stop, to turn, to run. One eye on the yawning hole before him, the darkness like a wall. He patted his pocket, sighed with a mix of relief and dread as he felt the blocky matchbox nestled there. He drew it out, lit a match, and flicked it inside the tunnel. The dark wall exploded into light, the mote of brilliant flame arcing slightly and then landed just past his satchel, the small fire throwing back the darkness some length behind it.

Raw, torn, and bloodied, the thief once more entered the tunnel, the sound of rushing water dying to a faint hiss behind him. He crawled forward, lit another match, and flicked it as far as he could further up the tunnel. Nothing but silent stone and darkness.

He pilfered what he could from the varied heap, judging worth and cost at a glance, nudging what he deemed less worthy aside, ignoring his tools altogether, one eye always on the tunnel. Beneath it all was the spice pouch. It was a little torn, but its contents were still nestled within, glimmering like reddish-brown gold in the meager firelight. Finn let loose a breath he hadn't realized he had been holding.

And then all went dark, and he heard a guttural, garbled voice say, "Ah, there you are."

In the dark distance, golden irises came alive with a hellish internal light, burning rings too wide in the crushing darkness.

The stink of hot breath filled the tunnel. The rings came closer, swinging forward in strange bounds without a sound, hungry and intent. They and the thing that owned them would be on him in seconds, it was simple math. There was no time to crawl away.

With a scream, Finn snatched the flatbow from the depths of the torn roll, his fingers tight around its leather grip. He was a terrible shot, there was no denying that. Much like how an artist made for a lousy laborer, he, a talented thief, made for a lousy boltman. But in a tunnel less than four feet across, even a blind man could land something. Finn aimed at those rings of light like targets, and pulled the trigger. The arrow flew true, whistling in the cramped confines and plunged into the thing's right iris, shutting it forever. But there was no wounded howl, no angry snarl. Only an amused laugh, the remaining iris shadowed into a golden crescent by a smiling cheek.

"A fighter..." it said airily, no longer sounding like the enraged guard that had chased him before, but cold and alien. "We'll set you right. Once you see what I have seen, all will be forgiven."

The remaining eye widened to a golden plate, that mysterious flicker of light playing again in its depths. A most curious thing, like stars at the bottom of a well, shimmering, spelling out something. Finn knew, somehow he *knew*, that he could read them if he looked hard enough, parcel their meaning with the right tilt of his head...

Pain, worse than the thief had ever known, ripped through his outstretched hand (when had he reached forward?!), as if it had been wrapped in a coil of barbed wire. Reaction took over, he tried to pull away, but the pain rose in pitch, ballooning into unreal agony. All he could do was howl and watch as that pit of hellfire, now within reach of him, drew closer, the beasts growls of anticipation clammy and damp against his face. The image was too much, the pain was too much. Finn screamed, tossed everything he could at the thing, all the hard-earned treasure he had risked his life for, until the only thing he had left was the spice.

For one, fleeting moment, the image of his father's face appeared in his mind—before being banished by another jolt of white-hot pain.

Finn threw the pouch.

The creature's mad huffing stopped, replaced with a grunt of surprise, then a tearing of leather. And, finally, a series of viscous coughs. Fine dust and spittle sprayed Finn's face with each hacking expulsion, mingling with the tears that were already there. The warm woody smell of the spice filled his nostrils and coated his mouth, suffocating and cloying.

And then, to Finn's amazement, the clawed hand that had gripped him like a vice loosened, and then retreated entirely. He did not waste the opportunity.

Crawling backwards as best he could, his right hand and part of his forearm all but useless, he kept his gaze fixed straight ahead, waiting for that golden ring to open and bear down on him. But the creature was still preoccupied, hacking and spitting with every breath like it had contracted the grippe.

Finn's feet touched empty air and once more, he slipped out into the open, this time falling backwards into the sand in a bloodied heap.

He stumbled to his feet, one arm holding the other tight to his chest, adrenaline fighting the fire burning in his hand. He didn't want to look at it, but he forced himself. It was indeed a ruin; the fingers broken and twisted, set in unnatural angles, long claw marks raking his forearm, sticky black blood everywhere.

Seems like an awful lot of blood... Finn thought, but only distantly, the way one might wonder if their porridge had gone cold.

It didn't seem real to Finn: the hideous wound, the blood, all of it. It was as if he were witnessing someone else's misfortune in a dream, remote and separate from himself. The sound of scratching claws inside the tunnel snapped him out of his shock like a slap of cold water, and he ran toward the sluice gate, mangled hand forgotten.

River spray coated the gate's surface, the constant barrage of the Korinthar wearing it down into a brittle crossing of oxidized iron that proved easy enough to break through with a simple shove of his good shoulder.

On the other side was a small wooden dock, empty but for undone ropes listing haphazardly in the churning water. Of the boat, if ever there had been one, there was no sign. To his right, stairs stretched upward to a stone landing, soft white light spilling over its edge. The stairs were wet, slippery, but Finn pounded up the steps all the same, wincing with every lunge, gasping at every slip, his balance thrown from the arm he kept clasped tight against his chest.

Near the apex, the path curved slightly and opened up into a neglected gazebo wreathed in vines and weeds. Ahead was the hedged yard he had traipsed through what seemed like a lifetime ago. The chateau once again loomed, its bland, brutalist facade like an obscene joke in its contrast to the nightmares it hid.

The stark black windows stared out at him as he ran, watching his flight with what felt like hungry interest. The acute throbbing in his arm was simmering down into a stabbing ache, but the wound continued to weep blood, staining the ground behind him. He knew he wouldn't last much longer.

Blearily, he reached for the gate at the edge of the manor grounds—the one leading back to the city. To Finn's surprise, it was ajar, the bar that had fastened it shut, tossed aside. He didn't know when that had happened and didn't much care, pushing against the gate with abandon. He put all his weight into the endeavor, but the gate swung open more easily than he'd been expecting, and he wound up falling to his knees on the cobblestones outside. Despite the cuts and the broken bones, he hardly felt a thing.

Tears streamed down his face, wracking sobs filling his chest at the relief he felt there upon the muddied ground.

"Hey now!"

Finn looked up and froze in place as a contingent of redjackets, rifles in arm, swarmed him. It was impossible to tell their number, the lightpost behind them casting them into vague shadows, but there was no mistaking the uniform or the shape of their high felt hats.

Finn raised his good hand over his face, as much to show the militia he meant no harm as to take shelter from the blaring light.

"Stay still you bastard, unless you want a ball between your eyes," the same rough voice said, and this time, Finn noted the hint of underlying fear in the command, the cadence too high and shrill. "Take your hands off your face."

"Just shoot him and be done with it, corporal," a different voice growled, and a chorus of others agreed with him.

Ignoring them, the corporal said, gentler this time, "Show us your eyes, son."

Finn did so, since whatever he'd survived, a lead ball would end him just the same. "P-please sir, there's something after me, it—" he rasped.

"Quiet," the corporal grunted.

The barrel of a rifle came into view, filling Finn's vision, the mouth inches from his face, close enough to look like a yawning pit. He tensed. But no belching fire came from the barrel, no lead ball flashed through his brain. Instead, the barrel moved across his forehead, parting the long hair that had come loose. Through the glare, Finn could see the corporal more clearly, an ashen-faced man who looked to be in his thirties, yet had lines creasing his forehead and cheeks, and gray hairs intermingled with brown. His gaze was critical, merciless.

The moment stretched, seconds akin to hours for Finn, who could do nothing but wait for his sentencing.

The corporal grunted and lifted him up effortlessly by the collar of his jerkin before throwing him bodily into the arms of two surprised redjackets. "Take him to the triage to see that wound. Then throw 'em in chains."

Perhaps it was the blood loss, the constant strain of the night, or his mental capacity pulled to its limit—but Finn struggled to find a more wonderful set of words. The two officers gave their best salute, leaden with Finn's own dead weight, before one hauled the thief to his feet. The other made to take the lead before his eyes went huge and he raised his rifle.

Finn jerked out of the way—more of a wince, exhausted as he was—but the shot wasn't meant for him. There was a strangled scream and chorus of alarmed shouts just behind. The redjacket holding Finn promptly dropped him, reaching for his own weapons.

The thief hit the ground hard, landing on his maimed arm with a sickening squelch and crack of bone. He groaned, turning himself sideways toward the gate, drawn by the rising shouts and igniting gunpowder. In the center of that maelstrom, bordered by desperate redjackets unloading round after round of lead and fire, was the creature. Its shape was obscured by the gunsmoke, but the shadows within spoke to some monstrous shape Finn would never have mistaken for human. It flailed and kicked with misshapen limbs, sending many of the gear-ladened enforcers sailing through the air. Through it all, the single golden ring burned, ever trained on the thief.

There was a shout just above Finn's shoulder, a glint of glass in the air, and suddenly the night came alive with an eruption of fire that engulfed the creature in an instant. It danced and swayed in apparent distress, its movements more akin to an insect set alight than a living man. It pirouetted once, lunged at the dazed corporal, taking him into a fiery, crushing embrace before collapsing into a smoldering heap.

The remaining soldiers, a third of their original number, stared numbly at the carnage, with one unloading a superfluous round of ammunition into the smoking carcass, presumably making sure the thing was truly dead. Amidst the smoke and the burning flesh, Finn caught the smell of the spice—that warm and woody aroma, amplified and improved by the flame, honed into its purest form by the crucible of fire.

It sickened him, flooding his mouth with spit like he was about to retch. Finn turned his eyes away, trying to breathe through his mouth, instead. Yet still, he could taste the spice on his tongue.

He struggled to his feet, cradling his arm once again. The redjackets looked to him and then one another, evidently unsure of what to do now that their corporal was carved to pieces. They watched Finn as he stumbled away, none raising any kind of objection nor threat as he rounded a corner and was gone from sight.

He wasn't sure where he was going; the alleys seemed strange to him, unfamiliar, despite having walked them dozens of times before. Night was full on, the sparse street lamps mostly unlit, yet still, pockets of orange light from uncontrolled fires bursting from store fronts and the back windows of houses illuminated the way. Dazed citizens wandered the street, some blood soaked, others missing entire limbs or swathes of flesh, lifeless bodies appearing in their midst periodically. Gunfire and screams drifted through the air, almost drowned by the roar of distant flames, growing more frequent with each passing minute. Madness wherever Finn turned, the nightmare that had pursued him in the manor spilling out into the rest of the city.

He stopped in front of an apothecary shop to catch his breath. His head was swimming, the smell of the spice still filling his nostrils, nearly making him sick again.

Something caught his eye, a glint, a small movement within the door's threshold, accompanied with the overwhelming feeling of being watched. Would those eyes be gold, their irises filled with that bewitching light? He did not wait to find out, sprinting from that entrance in full flight, not caring where or to what he was going.

He didn't last long after that. His limbs were getting heavy, his sight blurring along its edges, turning shadows and contrasting lights into every kind of nightmare he could imagine, most with grinning mouths and yellow eyes.

In the end, he found shelter in an abandoned tanner's shop, the interior dusty and strewn with forgotten instruments. The stairs leading to the second floor fared little better, cracking hideously with every step. Yet still they held, spilling out into a small apartment that opened up to a landing where still more stairs ascended to the rooftop. Finn took them, some thoughts about getting his bearings jumbled with a general desire to get away from the chaos below—and collapsed near the top, utterly spent.

He settled, holding his mangled arm tight. It still ached to high hell, but the bleeding had stopped and he thanked the Saint for that. Below and before him the slums of lower Elsed burned, the singular pyre that had only hours before smoldered neatly in its heart now roaring well beyond its limits. Patrolmen scrambled in force through the streets, rifles blasting periodically into the forms of shambling figures that, from a distance, could have been human. Or not.

Finn watched them, numb, no longer smiling at the chaos and disorder but desperately wishing for its end. He gripped himself tighter and shivered despite the heat, his eyes growing heavy. He'd rest there for a while and after that... After that, he wasn't so sure, but whatever came next, one thing was certain: his days as a thief were over.

—

Luis Alamo-Rivera asked his girlfriend to write this bio for him, because he is, at the moment, too busy possibly drowning in the ocean. When he's not doing that, he spends most of his time telling people who cough up blood that they should consider stopping, but they aren't always convinced. He erroneously prefers sci-fi over fantasy, but is pretty much immaculate in every other way, plus he has great taste in women. Please do not speak to him, or else he won't stop talking and will never get any writing done.

A Baby Cthulhu Bedtime Story

By Cooper D. Barham

Naomi couldn't help but believe in the old god Cthulhu...seeing as he slept in a small, luxurious dog kennel at the foot of her bed. Cthulhu, the ancient, tentacled Lovecraftian horror, was remarkably cute at one one-thousandth of his natural size and strength. Naomi was especially fond of the gurgling noise he made when excited, and the vague, distant siren of madness that one heard when staring into his eyes.

He was adorable.

The deli on 7th Avenue was having a lunch special, so Naomi decided to try and take her marine menace into public. She reasoned that he wasn't likely to learn any manners if he was stuck inside all day.

"*Hey*," she caressed the little beast's leathery, lumpy skull, her tone placating. "Buddy. Try not to drive anybody to the doors of insanity this time, okay?"

Cthulhu contemplated a nearby cocker spaniel with his black, globular eyes.

"Ah. No dogs, either."

Cthulhu grumbled, a couple of his face tentacles curling like burned paper.

"Stop that," Naomi kneeled and handed him his favorite toy boat. "Let's eat. Do you want the turkey and bacon? Dijon pastrami?"

Cthulhu's attention held to the dog as it sat beneath the table of a nearby family, waiting for fate to reward its patience with some displaced cut of ham.

Naomi snapped her fingers. "Kid, focus. Sandwiches."

Cthulhu stamped his feet, seafoam frothing at his mouth. Naomi hated to admit it, but he was most cuddly when he was a little upset.

Sighing, she addressed the worker behind the deli bar, a young man in his early twenties with a head of hair that looked like he could be on a volumizing conditioner billboard. He was ashen as he gazed at the cold-blooded Eldritch nightmare, voice wavering as he spoke. "Why can I hear my mother screaming?"

"Oh, don't worry about that," Naomi dismissed him with a wave. "Two reubens, please."

Once seated at their table—Cthulhu was in a kiddie seat—Naomi made her way through the savor of a well-made reuben, while her little tentacled baby boy prodded curiously at his own.

With her free hand, Naomi scrolled unceremoniously through a litany of half-formed men on that month's chosen dating app, avoiding any messages from people who wore red flags on their sleeves. (And avoiding some of them, notably, a second time. Nothing worse than a guy who became volatile after not receiving a response within a few hours). Finding a diamond in the rough was hard work.

Definitely not Troy, 28, flexing his six-pack abs. Show-off.

Absolutely not Damian, 29. He had a house, which was a pretty enticing option, except his sense of interior design was awful. Who put a lime green accent wall in the same room as burnt orange upholstery? And a *water bed?* Pass.

Hard skip on Tyler, 30. No Tylers ever again. Why did Tylers even exist? Who invented Tylers?

Naomi stopped mid-bite, eyes falling on a modestly appetizing morsel of a man, with a decent hairline, reasonable fashion sense, and a wonderful picture with a woman whom Naomi assumed had to be his mother, based on their shared, eerily beautiful white-blue eyes. Recessive genes for the win.

Mont, 27. Huh.

Naomi usually liked them a bit older, but...

"Hey," she said, holding the phone screen to baby Cthulhu, who was tearing through some corned beef. "Does he look cute to you?"

Incoherent garbles of playful violence.

"Sick, thanks for the input," she said, and then swiped an affirmative.

Mont arrived right on time at the local overpriced Mexican restaurant, El Gordo Poblano (the syntax error identifying it as resolutely American). Overpriced, because Naomi wanted to test the man's mettle. His dedication, his gumption. She would throw him against the gauntlet of a $22.99 chimichanga and see if he had the audacity to pursue her further.

"Good evening," he said, cordial. He wore a simple gray button-up and had his neat, sandy-blond hair combed to the side. He looked like he was a financial advisor or something boring like that. "Is this seat taken?" He gestured to the seat obviously meant for him.

Ha. Ha ha. Corny joke. Points deducted.

From her own seat, Naomi creased her lips into something so reserved it barely counted as a smile and laughed once as a courtesy. "It is, if you're my bounty hunter rendezvous," she leaned in, conspiratorially lowering her voice. "Is the target...well, you know."

It only took Mont a beat to catch her flow. "We don't talk about the, uh," he mimed slitting his throat with his thumb, "*clients* in public."

Wow. Naomi wasn't expecting him to actually keep up with that. Points refunded. Also, that was too smooth; he might actually be a serial killer.

"Code name: Naomi," she said.

"Code name: Mont," he answered.

Huh. Not bad, Mont. Not bad.

Together, they ordered off the menu, each of them speaking in turn—an improvised cipher nobody understood. They were just riffing. Thus, *chicken burrito* or *enchiladas de pollo* became an order of "failed dinosaur wrapped in deflated bread, covered by milk that went to war."

Their poor server had no idea what was happening.

About fifteen minutes later, they hit *the moment.*

"Okay, I figure it's best to get this out of the way early," Mont said as Naomi was literally only one bite into her chimichanga.

C'mon man, not yet, she thought. *Let me at least get halfway through the meal before you reveal you breed praying mantises or have spontaneous explosive diarrhea syndrome or whatever.*

And she knew it was gonna be big, because he paused, shifting his weight back and forth in his seat, gathering up courage for whatever came next. Great.

Then he started unbuttoning his shirt.

Oh god, did he have a tumor? He was dying, wasn't he? Or was it a living teratoma with a name? A teratoma named Prince Lester. How could she hope to be titillating with a man who would title any manner of toothy tumor?

But it wasn't a clump of expanding cells he revealed, it was the t-shirt underneath. A shirt that showed...

"Oh my god," Naomi involuntarily brought a couple fingers to her temple, her mouth hanging ajar, melted cheese dangling from her bottom lip.

His black t-shirt showed a graphic in the styling of an old science fiction book, depicting a certain eldritch deity crashing ships against a rocky shore, the tentacles on his face revealed by a lone lighthouse beacon.

"I—" Mont cleared his throat. "I believe in cosmic beings beyond our understanding, and await the day that their primordial violence would purify our world in blood, carnage, and the madness of the space between stars! All hail the Old Ones. All hail their imminent sovereignty. All hail."

Then, having exposed what seemed to be his greatest vulnerability, Mont sat down and awaited her judgment.

Naomi finished her bite of chimichanga and placed her fork on the table, dabbing her mouth with a napkin.

She leaned forward, peering into his eyes.

"Bro," she said. "You're not gonna believe this."

When Naomi took Mont back to her apartment, she imagined the expression he would have upon seeing his god in the living flesh. What was in one moment an idea he believed in fiercely, and hoped for, and dreamt about, would suddenly be sitting across from them in the same material dimension, upside-down, in a diaper, kicking its feet while watching Paw Patrol and eating *sketty* and meatballs.

She imagined how everything about Mont would be slack, his words stuttering like an old motorboat engine that could die any minute. He would be bewildered. Reality would become incomprehensible, the void of nihilism surrounding all of humankind magnified and folded upon itself, crashing down upon his shoulders, threatening to blot out his mind in one final blast of cognitive unraveling.

None of that happened, because Cthulhu was not in her apartment, and Mont was very unimpressed.

Not too unimpressed to leave, though. Perhaps his hope that Naomi was telling the truth—that Cthulhu was there, in her home, and enjoyed premium dog food with scrambled eggs—was enough to keep him hoping.

"Well, shit," Naomi said, examining the latch of her door. When tested, she realized it hadn't locked as well as she'd believed it had. Shitty apartment. "This isn't good."

"I'll admit," Mont sighed while pacing her living room, looking around, "this is the most unusual way anyone has ever asked me to come home with them, especially on a first date," he paused in front of her bedroom door. "But you got me here, so are we gonna do this?"

Naomi was so zeroed-in on her child's absence that she almost missed that Mont was talking at all. "What's that? *Oh!* Ha, no. Now I need you to focus, because we have a serious problem."

"Problem?"

"Yeah," Naomi scanned underneath her bed. "Last time this happened, he was gone for three hours. By the time I found him, they were already building a new wing onto the local psychiatric hospital for everyone left in his wake."

"Uh-huh."

"They got better" she cleared her throat. "But we should avoid it as much as possible, you know? Can I count on you to help?"

At that, Naomi could tell she activated something inside Mont. It flashed in his eyes—someone needed him. Was choosing to rely on him. His uncertainty evaporated and he straightened up, taking on a sharpened disposition.

Aww, was his sense of value dependent on his usefulness to others, and she was providing an opportunity for him to fill a long-unaddressed emotional need? Cute!

She nodded. "First, the laundry room. He likes staring into the washing machines. Something about dark whirlpools soothes him."

Cthulhu was not in the laundry room. Nor was he on the playground. Nor was he ripping open the delicate seams between dimensions behind the maintenance shed. That happened once, after Naomi forgot to feed him. Buddy could get *hangry*.

They caught his trail after visiting the dog park. Every canine present—from pitties to german shepherds to a french bulldog named Bark Twain—was cowering, whimpering, and too terrified to move. Little living statues, shaking and peeing uncontrollably.

That turned Naomi's insides a bit. At the end of the day, her baby boy *was* a mind-bending dark entity from beyond the veil of reality.

Discerning his motivations, instincts, and needs was a difficult undertaking. Naomi liked to think that, in his relative innocence, Cthulhu didn't intend to harm these dogs...but she couldn't say that for sure. Even playing with him was dangerous.

For everyone but her, anyway.

Still, after asking the owners of said dogs where Cthulhu had gone, Naomi had no leads, and that was when the fretting really started to set in.

"Naomi," Mont grabbed her by the arm to keep her from pacing the pavement into slag. "I have an idea. Follow me."

So she did, allowing him to lead her to a brick pedestrian bridge that crossed over a nearby river.

Unbeknownst to Naomi, that day was the city's annual remote-control boat race. Until that moment, she thought those were fake. She'd only ever seen one in *Stuart Little 2*. Yet, forty local contestants had shown up to pit their distantly piloted aquatic vessels in a battle of speed and strategic maneuvering.

At least, that's what was supposed to happen.

Instead, Naomi and Mont surveyed the chaos as dozens of miniature boats sped toward shore, desperately hoping to escape the infantile wrath of baby Cthulhu in the midst of his self-appointed playtime.

They watched as Cthulhu snuck beneath the dark waters in one part of the river, only to either pull a boat down below the surface, never to be seen again, or to lurch up out of the water and crash into the craft, rending it into debris.

Naomi would be so proud and delighted at her boy's creativity and joy, if it weren't for all the owners of those boats screaming profanities at him.

"Hold this," Naomi said, unzipping her jacket and shoving it into Mont's arms.

"Hold it for what?"

But she'd already jumped off the bridge into the river, his words trailing behind her.

It was a quick descent—no more than twenty feet—before she was subsumed by a cool, murky dark.

Naomi's head broke the river's surface a moment later. "Baby boy! Buddy!" she shouted, paddling toward what she thought was his last-known location. "Munchkin, we gotta go home! You're upsetting lots of people."

The river wasn't especially wide, nor was Cthulhu especially covert with his destruction. Naomi caught him capsizing a beautiful, multi-sail ship, clutching a fistful of mast and body-slamming it into the depths. Which was impressive in a way, since it was twice his size.

Naomi wrapped an arm around him from behind and started to swim furiously toward the nearest shore. Cthulhu thrashed for a moment before realizing it was her, then his resistance turned to glee—which gave Naomi cause for relief. She had worried he was going to make things more difficult than necessary.

When a moment later they reached solid land, Mont was waiting to help pull them free of the water.

Apologies to the boat owners ensued, as well as promises of reimbursement for the several ships that were victim to playtime. This little debacle would put Naomi back a few months in paying off her student loans. (Meaning now it would only take twenty years and a few months. Yaaay.)

An hour later, they were back at Naomi's apartment and Mont had an opportunity to properly gape at what he'd just done and seen—yep, that was actually Cthulhu and yep, he did nap with a polka-dot blankie—Naomi made coffee for the two of them.

"I still can't believe it," Mont sat, head in his hands.

"Wild stuff, I know," Naomi handed him a mug.

"I...don't know what to do with this knowledge," Mont's mouth moved up and down, like a fish out of water. "He's so cute. What the shit. He's not supposed to be cute."

"Isn't defying mortal expectations and comprehension his whole deal? Don't think about it too hard," She sat down next to Mont. "Just listen to that snore."

It *was* an adorable snore, his little tentacles vibrating and furling as he scratched his leathery skull with one hand before turning over.

"Hang around long enough and you'll learn to appreciate it," Naomi said, holding up her mug.

Mont blinked, clicked the lip of his mug against hers, and sighed. "We'll see."

"So I guess that means date number two is next weekend?"

He smiled. "I'll date you or go mad trying."

—

Cooper D. Barham is truly, completely clueless. Honestly, it's a miracle he's made it this far. In spite of himself, he keeps trying to do things, and through the combined efforts of awesome people like those in this anthology, occasionally it works out. He'd be nothing without them. Just a puddle of energy drinks, sad video game music, and leftover hair from his corgi.

You can find his other published work, "Each and Every Phantom," on Amazon, as well as visit his Substack newsletter, "Arcane Daydream", where he spends entirely too much time formulating strong opinions about media you probably don't care about.

Each and Every Phantom

Substack

This Wonderful Place

By John Jacob

I wake up again in This Wonderful Place. Angel Derrick is vacuuming the grass. Angel José is in the spirit food house. He gives me my spirit foods in a paper cup. There is a pink diamond, a white pearl, and a capsule of fine sand. There is also The Raindrop and The Emerald. I swallow them and show Angel José my empty mouth and cup, so he knows that I liked them.

I go to The Garden to do nothing. I go to The Garden to do nothing every day.

Benedict is there. He is sitting in a lawn chair, facing The Lake. He and I have both seen The Lake enough times to have it memorized, so there is no special reason to sit looking at it now. But every chair has to point somewhere, or else it is a stool. I pull up a chair to sit next to Benedict.

"I had a dream last night," he says, "I got close to The Lake. Closer than ever. It was enormous."

I stand up and walk toward The Lake until my nose touches it. It almost fills my vision, and my head covers it in shadow.

"Not like that," he continues. I sit back down and wipe the dust off my nose. "It was bigger than The Garden. Your whole body could have gone inside it. The surface moved, too, like the top of a glass of water when you blow on it."

Most of my dreams are about This Wonderful Place. I never want to leave, even when I am asleep. It is perfect. But, sometimes, in my dream, I am back in The World. The sun there is burning and relentless. It hurts my skin and eyes. It is a circle, white, black, blue, and orange, all at once. When you look away, you still see it looking into you. I feel the presence of The Demon behind me. It reaches an invisible talon toward me, but is stopped by the glassy wall of The Emerald. The Raindrop is there, tall as a tower. It opens up, and water rushes out and destroys The Whole World in a flood. My body is buoyed back up to the surface, where I float beneath a gentle sun of flickering orange until the waters shrink and they are The Lake and I am in The Garden back in This Wonderful Place.

And then—

I wake up again in This Wonderful Place. Angel Derrick is vacuuming the grass. Angel José is in the spirit food house. He gives me my spirit foods in a paper cup. There is a pink diamond, a white pearl, and a capsule of fine sand. There is also ____________ and ____________. I look questioningly at Angel José.

"You're good. Doctor says you're ready," he says.

I am without words. There is not The Raindrop that Drowns The World. Nor is there The Emerald that Makes The Demon Sleep.

I go to The Garden to do nothing. Instead, I worry.

I sit next to Benedict. His chair is pointing the same way as yesterday. Every chair has to point somewhere, or else it is a stool.

"The Cloud was moving," he said. He is talking about a dream, because The Cloud never moves. It is up and a little to the right of the lake, where it goes. It is perfect. "It was moving very slowly, like it had been thrown. But slowly."

He'd had a dream about The World. In The World, every cloud moves slowly in search of This Wonderful Place. None of those clouds will ever find it, because they are of The World, and they are lost. In The World, also, sometimes the demons throw things. Demons can throw things, but neither Benedict nor I could ever throw anything.

A long time ago, close to when I first came to This Wonderful Place, The Demon was always in control. It did not understand that This Wonderful Place is perfect. It did not even believe that it is wonderful. It paced the floor impatiently. It pretended to eat the spirit foods and spat them out later. It went to The Library and read books about The World, and imagined it was back in The World.

One day, it threw a book at Angel Derrick and tried to run out of This Wonderful Place. Angel José tackled it and used The Needle to make The Demon sleep. With The Demon asleep, I was free again.

Angel Dr. Gabriel invites me to a meeting. He does not wear white, but he is still an angel.

"I think you have been doing very well," he says.

"Thank you," I say.

"And you have been here for a very, very long time."

"Thank you," I say.

Angel Dr. Gabriel thinks for several seconds. Then he says, "I think you are ready to go back to The World."

The Demon splashes in my belly, like a fish.

In my dream, I am back in The World. The sun is burning and relentless. I feel the presence of The Demon behind me. The Emerald is not there. Its invisible talon reaches into my back, where there is an invisible opening, like it was unzipped. It slides its legs into my own legs like it is putting on pants. Its fingers go into my own, like gloves. Its eyes, tongue, mind, and feelings all wear my own, like garments never before imagined or named. Its legs carry me toward a sepulcher of glass and brick. A door yawns which The Demon and I know will close, and will not open for anyone but Time.

And then—

I wake up again in this place. I hear vacuuming.

The nurse gives me what remains of my regimen. It is probably still helping. I want the green pill and the blue pill.

I go to the library. My head is foggy. It is hard to care about what any of the books say.

I go to the TV room. One of the residents is sitting behind the couch, gazing at the mural painted on the opposite wall: a green garden, a yellow path snaking up to the horizon, a lake, a cloud. When I have my green pill and my blue pill in me, I think he and I get along well.

I sit on the couch and watch TV. People are wearing costumes. They are embroiled in a high-stakes scenario. They will be fine in half an hour. Blackout. A woman has a clever and triumphant look on her face as she brushes her teeth. A closeup of the toothbrush she was using, posed upright next to its packaging. A cheeseburger takes the place of the toothbrush. It rotates, slowly, then a montage rapidly fires burger shots at different angles. The juices glisten. Suddenly, the bottom bun is alone at the foot of the frame. Ingredients descend, one by one, onto that foundation: lettuce leaf, tomato slice, onion circle, meat puck, cheese square, puck #2, cheese the second, two pickle slices—the cross sections always looked like faces to me, although they don't really look like faces—drowned under a waterfall of ketchup, mayonnaise, and mustard; sesame seed lid. All of this temptation, but there are exactly two things that I want. There is another blackout, and the people in the costumes are back.

Make that three things I want. The first two are green and blue. The third would be to walk out those doors in my confiscated shoes, with my pants held high by my confiscated belt.

I get up and go back to the nurse. I tell him I am having withdrawal, an emergency. He calls the doctor and hands me the phone and the doctor asks me on a scale of one to ten if my withdrawal is bad, and I say eleven. The nurse gets the phone back and gives me my half-emerald and my lovely miniature sapphire. I swallow them and The Cloud of Bliss hisses out of my pores, and I sleepwalk to my bed to dream of The Garden.

Morgan and Ferris have come to This Wonderful Place. I had forgotten them, but I remember them now.

They walk on the vacuumed grass with their shoes on. Ferris looks in the spirit food house. He asks Angel José if his old fashioned is any good. They act excited to see me. Morgan hugs me. Ferris grabs my hand, and then hugs me.

They look around at this place as if it is not truly wonderful. I am above feeling scorn, however, because of the power of This Wonderful Place. Morgan looks at me.

"You're really going to miss it here, huh?" she asks.

I go to Angel Dr. Gabriel.

"The Demon inside me is awake," I say. "It woke up when I didn't take The Emerald and The Sapphire."

"The what?" he asks.

"I didn't have The Emerald and The Sapphire the day before last, and the next morning, The Demon woke up and took control."

"Ah. It is normal to be nervous about getting back to The World when you have been here a long time," he says.

I try to let The Demon take control while everyone and the strong angels are here, so they can see the danger and the evil.

But The Demon does nothing. It sits coiled in my belly like a snake, and sleeps.

All of my things go into bags brought by Morgan and Ferris.

There is only one thing I can desire, and that is to stay in This Wonderful Place. By the power of this place, I am unwrathful, but in my mind I am aware of what my wrath would be, were I a demon. I would scream at Morgan and hit Ferris and put my things back where they go.

By the power of this place, I am compliant. I follow them to where Angel José gives me the belt and shoes I was wearing when I first arrived.

The World is burning and blinding, and it hurts my skin and eyes. The sun of this place punishes all, always, for the first transgression. My hair moves. Everything moves: the trees, the grass, the air, all yearning for escape; not knowing there exists A Wonderful Place to escape to, right there, disguised as glass and brick.

The car is as hot as an oven. It stinks of gluttony and oily paper. It moves fast. I had forgotten anything could move this fast. We go very far, very fast, and I become lost. The World is bloated with size, and a desperate confusion of things which lack all knowledge of the perfection they imitate.

My stomach sinks, down, down: an ocean trench. The Abyss stirs in The Demon's ebbing slumber. Its eyes open like full moons gazing out of the deep. A talon breaches the surface and slides into my arm, into my fingers. It makes its raiment of my body. Its eyes, tongue, mind, and feelings all wear my own like garments unimagined and unnamed. My thoughts are cut off from the source; the last drops out of a faucet. They are The Demon's unwelcome memories, now. I feel The Demon's happiness and relief. Ferris turns and looks back. He smiles. The Demon smiles back, with the face that was mine.

And—

I come back to this wonderful place.

—

John Jacob was raised in rural Southern Maryland, where he learned to love the Chesapeake Bay, low light pollution, and being 30 minutes away from the nearest McDonalds. He studied Liberal Arts At Bard College at Simon's Rock, where he received his A.A., and Chinese Language and Literature at University of Maryland College Park, where he dropped out.

In 2016, he began his Software Engineering career with no qualifications except for a caffeine-shaped hole above his chin, and a skull full of woodland rodents. John's literary style consists of desperately trying to finish anything at all that looks like a story.

The Manifesto of an Unhinged Pigeon

By J.L. Zhang

BEHOLD human,
    you stand before a
    descendant of
    the MOST FEARED

Back then, WE ROAMED THE EARTH
    with our legendary brethren,
    now bones in poorly lit museums
    we accidentally fly into.

Just as our ancestors LAY WASTE to
    the vast expanse of the land,
    so do we, on your shiny new Teslas.

Though we are smaller now, and
    our brains equally reduced,
    We demand FREEDOM to rule the sky
    without slamming into your
    corporate cages, because your window washer
    was a try-hard.

BEWARE

OUR MIGHT WILL RETURN
one picnic sandwich left
unattended at a time.

Every Cheeto you drop,
   every corn you pop,
   we'll be flocking.

—

J.L. Zhang grew up in Northern California, and like many of her invasive kin, currently resides in Austin. She is a designer by trade, has cavity-inducing proclivities, and hates writing in third-person.

August

By Anna Leah Karasik

I fall first. A warm wind shakes us and pulls the last fibers of my stem from the twig. The rustling of my kindred quietens as I flutter left, right, and down, down, down. I finally scratch to a stop on the grass, looking up. We're all exactly alike—supple and waxy, heads perfectly tapered into a lovely little point. Now they look so small and frantic up there.

For all my life, we've looked down at the people who sit in our shadow. We've done nothing but whisper and tease since sprouting out in unison. Now I lay flat, helpless, looking up at my counterparts—all of them still happy, green, alive.

This isn't a surprise. I've had an entire day to accept my fate: just one twist of the talon, and a bird untethered me from my lifeline. That beaked menace stole my nourishment, but more importantly, he stole me away from the others.

I felt the change almost instantly: one moment our veins ran rich with life, and the next...mine alone now squeezing shut, blackening from the inside out. I find myself wishing I'd savored our cacophonous gossiping, our blustery rain dances.

From here among our earthbound sisters, I can't understand their whispers—but I can finally feel the full force of the dancing sunlight we orchestrate. I can watch the whole shivering group sway gracefully as one, and appreciate how very many we are. *They* are.

I'm not us. I'm just me—a crisp thing that might crack and break under the next pair of squeaking shoes to stroll by.

Suddenly, a pressure at my sides—a rush of wind—a softer bed. I'm splayed out in someone's hand. I'm mortified as they scrutinize my dying form.

"So beautiful!"

—

In real life, Anna Leah Karasik loves to conjure smiles. In video games, Anna loves to hoard loot. In either case, she loves to cuddle kitties, play dress-up, and boss people around. After several years producing TV news and writing game reviews, she's dusting away the creative cobwebs to write uplifting stories.

Mirror

By Ocean Blouth

It sat in the corner of the shopping center. White, gray, and silver balloons hovered next to the entrance. Red and white signs announcing sales were stuck to the large windows. A banner hung from the roof, with the words "Grand Opening" printed on it in large, black text.

The sight caught Jackie's attention while she waited at the bus stop at the edge of the parking lot. It had been a long day on her feet and she wasn't eager to walk around even more. However, the presence of something new drew her in.

Inside, she was surprised to see how crowded the small shop was. The air buzzed with voices and the drum of footsteps as people moved between each other.

It wasn't packed, but the shop was decently occupied for only selling mirrors—not to mention, it was still early morning. Too curious to resist, Jackie moved through the nearest set of aisles, noting that a particular one was lined with small handheld mirrors. Rounded, square, elongated. All in different colors, some soft and pastel, others bright and bold.

Jackie didn't know how long the store had been open, but for there to be gaps in the shelves already was unusual. And as nice as some of the mirrors were, they were just that: mirrors. As Jackie moved around, she passed by a couple who were gazing into a mirror together. Her ears caught the faint sound of the two of them muttering to each other.

She brushed it off and continued browsing. There were several others who were staring into mirrors. Was there a special way to tell if one was good by looking at it from a certain angle? Was it like tapping a watermelon and listening to the sound?

Jackie walked between the shelves until she arrived at a section that displayed larger hanging mirrors. These were less colorful, yet their frames were more decorated with swirls, cross-hatches, and floral designs. She gravitated toward a silver-framed mirror. It was polished and didn't have a speck of dirt on it. Whoever had set the store up for the opening had taken great care that everything was nice and presentable.

Stooping down, Jackie admired one on a lower shelf. She stared at it for a moment, looking for any distortion in the reflective backing. Were the other customers she'd seen looking for scratches? That would make sense. Regardless, this one had none. Setting the mirror on the floor, it reached up to Jackie's waist. Surprisingly, it wasn't as heavy as it looked.

Turning it over, Jackie looked at the back, which appeared to be covered with brown butcher paper. Besides the barcode in the bottom corner, there wasn't anything but a black-inked symbol: two trapezoids mirroring each other with a diagonal line going through them. Was that the manufacturing logo? It was an odd one. Too simplified, Jackie thought. And no name underneath... Strange.

Satisfied with the mirror, she took it home. Jackie lived in a small studio apartment, with her bed and dining table taking up most of the floor space. The walls were occupied with shelves to store what few belongings couldn't fit in the closet. She would rearrange things to make wall space later. For the time being, Jackie set the mirror on the floor across the room.

Sitting on her bed, Jackie held out her phone, intent on taking a picture to show her friend. Aiming the camera at the mirror, Jackie paused. Her phone was far from a newer model, the camera normally capturing dull and blurred images. But this was the first time she'd seen it distort colors that weren't there.

Through the lens of the camera, the glass of the mirror was tinted green. Not only that, but there was also a static-like graininess to the image. It shifted like dust in the air whenever she moved the camera.

Assuming it was just the reflective lining on the back of the mirror, Jackie brushed it off and took the picture, anyway.

She looked at the mirror, happy she bought it. Jackie couldn't keep herself from staring into it. Maybe it was the way it sat, allowing her to see the ceiling at an odd angle. Jackie chuckled to herself, thinking of how she had a whole new perspective on her own world.

A simple mirror gave someone a whole new way to see their own world. It was a funny way to interpret reflections, but the more Jackie gazed into the glass, the more convinced she was that maybe that was exactly what she needed.

The more Jackie thought about it, the more she felt stuck. What if that was only because she was seeing things from one angle? Sure, she had a boring retail job, but at least she had a job. Not everyone was able to work. She had her own place and wasn't forced to share with loud, clutter-causing roommates.

But knowing that alone wasn't enough. Something had to be done. Jackie spent the rest of the evening brainstorming on what she could do for herself.

The next morning during the bus ride to work, Jackie stared into the glass at her own reflection. But it was unclear, blurred by the rattling glass and the flash of the traffic beyond, the scarred surface caked with dirt. She yearned for the flawlessness of her mirror at home.

Yet still, she watched herself, a reflection traveling through a place so much like her own, yet different. Once she stepped off the bus, where would her reflection self go? Would she travel somewhere better than a clothing store? Would she get to work at all? Was she off on some grand adventure that Jackie could only hope for, traveling by bus out of convenience rather than necessity?

What about the reflection of Jackie from the seat across from her? Was that one already married? Childless or with several little ones running around? Maybe that one had a home where she could have pets? Perhaps she owned a house and worked in an office?

With each reflection that caught her eye, Jackie envisioned a different scenario that could have been her life. That could be her life. The thoughts spun around her like the sides of a whirlpool, closing in on her until she could hardly remember where she was.

It was the squeal of the brakes that broke Jackie from the thoughts. She blinked at her own reflection. Her mind was hazy, like waking from a dream, and the scenarios in her head faded away as quickly as one. *I'm just tired*, she thought to herself while stepping off the bus.

At the department store, Jackie would normally be tasked with tidying up the front, resetting displays, restocking racks, and removing any misplaced clothes. But not that day. Someone had called in, so Jackie was reassigned to watch over the women's dressing rooms in the back.

Among all stations within the store, the dressing rooms were the worst to be stuck with. Clothes were strewn about. Clothing hangers were piled under benches or missing completely. Forgotten drinks, trash, and broken security tags littered the floors. From opening to closing, the dressing rooms were always a mess.

Jackie began by doing a quick sweep of each of the rooms. Broom and dustpan in hand, she swept up bits of crumpled paper and broken tags, and picked up discarded hangers.

She moved slowly, often finding herself distracted by the dressing room mirrors. Each room had three standing mirrors, two of which were angled inwards toward each other. None of them were as nice as the mirrors she'd seen in the shop the previous day, though.

The dressing room mirrors allowed shoppers to view themselves from three different angles—but that wasn't enough. Jackie didn't know how to put the feeling into words yet, but the new angles alone wasn't what she needed. For now, she couldn't do anything about it, and she settled on staring at the space over her shoulder.

An anti-theft sign was stuck in the wall behind her. In the mirror, the reversed red print was nothing more than a mix of lines and curves.

They had no meaning in the mirror. No purpose. Just turning them in a new direction erased their meaning, their history, their worth. They were nothing but scribbles. And yet, the wall was still a wall. And Jackie still stood there, watching.

The time between watching the mirrors felt like a dream. Jackie drifted from one dressing room to another, cleaning as she was supposed to. But the task was nothing but a blur, and she quickly found herself lost in the reflective glass.

Knocks from customers were the only things that broke her trance. How long had it been since the store opened? Jackie couldn't linger in one room for too long. But there was always one that needed to be cleaned, which was what made manning the dressing rooms so tiring. It wasn't so bad that day, though. At least she always had a mirror waiting for her.

Life outside the mirrors was dull. Always the same angles, the same perspective. Jackie wanted more, to see things differently. Yet, nothing ever came to mind. She decided that after work, she would visit the mirror store again. That's where she first had the question on whether to change things in her life, so maybe an answer would be there, too.

When she stepped through the doors, Jackie was shocked by the swarm of people moving about the small store. How could a store like this gather such a crowd after only one day?

Jackie pushed her way down the aisles, looking around shifting bodies for anything she could grab for herself. Most of the shelves were vacant. Determined not to leave empty handed, she settled on a hand mirror and a small circular one to hang on the wall.

When she got home that evening, she set the mirrors wherever they would fit on the walls. When she sat on the bed to gaze at the largest of the three, Jackie found that, at a certain angle, she could see all of them.

Reflection through reflection. In the small hanging mirror, visible through the top right corner of the mirror on the floor, she could see her room completely upside down. And from that, she could see the hand mirror propped up on a shelf. In it, she could see the back of her own head.

It fascinated Jackie how, with something so simple, she could see things she would never be able to see with her own eyes.

She went back to the shop the next day. By this time, the store had been able to restock some of their shelves and she was able to walk away with a pack of six square wall mirrors.

She thought about where she would put them. There were some old pictures of family she could take down. Sure, she'd miss seeing her departed grandmother's face every morning. But wasn't being reminded of the deceased every day a bit morbid, anyway? And it wasn't like she was throwing the pictures out. She'd still have them in the closet. She was focusing on the future, after all.

Once she was done setting up her new mirrors, Jackie felt less unsure. She sat on the floor, her back against the bed. She stared through the mirror on the floor across from her. Through it, she could see so many corners and angles. So many objects in the room all at once.

Somewhere, in the very back of her mind, Jackie knew the mirrors could show her more.

In the coming days, she always went back to the mirror shop after work. Sure, the department store she worked in sold mirrors, too. But those didn't give Jackie the same feeling when she looked into them. She wasn't sure what that feeling was. It drew her in. Captured her mind. Whatever it was, it made her stare into those mirrors for hours on end.

Sure, it probably wasn't healthy, but it wasn't hurting anyone, including herself. Yes, she had to rearrange her apartment a few times: throw a few things out or push them into the closet or under the bed. But who didn't need to do those things from time to time? People with more space than she had, that's who.

Besides, Jackie was proud of her mirror collection. Some people collected records or movie posters, and Jackie collected mirrors. There was nothing wrong with that. The light reflecting off of them made the small space brighter, even if it was a bit empty. But it made Jackie happy, and that was what mattered.

In just over two weeks, her once shelf-covered walls were replaced with shining mirrors. Mirrors too large to hang without preparation sat leaning on the wall. Above them were smaller pieces, set up with whatever hooks, nails, or sturdy push pins Jackie could find. Most were reused from the shelves.

Jackie sat on her bed. Body relaxed, she stared through the reflective glass. Though her gaze never shifted, she could see the whole room at once. Every corner. Every fiber of the carpet. Every part of the room was in sight, no matter where anything sat.

In each piece of glass, the bedroom sat at a different angle. A different reflection. A different way to see the world. A new perspective. One that was always there. Always existing just slightly off from what was normal. And through each of these reflections was a new experience.

Jackie could see it all.

And with her new perspective, she could understand what she had missed.

The mirrors were showing her everything. They'd always done that for people hadn't they? People were limited to only seeing ahead of them. But with a mirror, anyone's vision could be more than that.

Mirrors helped people see themselves: who they really were and who they wanted to be. The ones on cars helped people see others, to keep them safe or warn them of danger. Mirrors had helped people see the stars—places so far away that humans would never get to experience them firsthand. Places that were once trapped only in the imagination.

But that realization wasn't enough. Just knowing wasn't enough. Jackie wanted to experience it for herself.

She wasn't content with just standing by and observing, anymore. Jackie wanted to go beyond her world of static angles and limited points of view. She wanted to see things in a new way. In any way she wanted, as the mirrors did. After all, perspective was only limited to where one set their feet.

Jackie had been rooted in one point of view her entire life. She wanted a new one. How could she achieve that? She couldn't spend the rest of her life sitting in her room staring at her mirrors, no matter how much it fascinated her. It was still only one room. Jackie wanted to see much more than that.

There were only so many ways to look into a mirror.

What could she see if she looked not into a mirror, but out of one? The idea excited Jackie. However, the question was just that: a question. Thoughts in her head with no answers to them. She had no way to look out from the other side; it wasn't as if she could just crawl inside like an open window.

The realization that her new desires were at a standstill drained the energy from Jackie. Her mind was overworked and tired, and after a full day of work, so was her body. She needed rest; after all, she was only human.

Jackie laid down to sleep and gave her thoughts a much-needed rest.

But even in her sleep, Jackie would not be away from the mirrors. In a place of no color or light or darkness, mirrors surrounded her, frozen in place like falling rain. They hung in the air as shards, fractured and incomplete. Hovering and unmoving, they showed nothing but more shards beyond their glass.

She could not understand the meaning.

The shard became a wall. It stretched far into immeasurable heights and reached out with no end. And through it, Jackie could see only a wall behind her. Brown like butcher paper. It stood like a sheet that was pulled too tight. On it, like a form in the mist, was the giant logo for the mirror shop.

Jackie woke up feeling confused and hungry. She hadn't eaten since lunch the previous day. She thought about her dream over a bowl of cereal. *Am I going crazy?* she wondered to herself. Surely her dream was just her brain telling her that she was obsessing over mirrors too much.

Looking over her small apartment, seeing the mirrors everywhere, she had to admit that it had all gone too far. She needed to get her head on straight.

Getting ready for work, Jackie stood in her bathroom. Pulling a washcloth from her face, she glanced at her reflection. Nothing about it had changed. Her eyes drifted around the glass, searching for anything out of place.

She found nothing.

The lure that had been behind the glass was gone. Had she done something wrong?

No. No, this was a good thing. Whatever had been wrong with her over the last week was over. She could go back to normal.

On the ride to work, she scrolled through social media, watching any video and reading any post or comment that she came across—anything to distract herself from the nagging in her head to gaze in the reflection next to her. When she got off the bus, she kept her head down, and did the same when she boarded later that day, doing her best to keep her eyes off the mirror store and drowning her desire to visit it again.

Over the next few days, things returned to normal. The dressing room mirrors at work no longer held the same magic as the day before. Why would they? They only showed a copy of a room Jackie was already in. Backward writing didn't change that.

Mirrors were back to being just mirrors. As they should be.

Had she just lost her mind over the last few days? Maybe her building had a gas leak that was fixed recently. It *would* be like her landlord not to mention something like that.

Either way, Jackie was glad that it was over.

She went back to her normal work of keeping the front of the store in order, all the while her dream replayed in her head. A wall made of a mirror. Was that meant to mean something or was a dream just that? Jackie wanted to believe there was something more.

It didn't matter, though, she thought to herself. She was better off leaving it alone and forgetting what happened.

That was hard to do once she was back at home, seeing as her apartment was covered with mirrors. The endless reflections gave her no answer as to what made her act the way that she had. What changed? She laid on her back, staring at the ceiling. Above Jackie was her own reflection. And beyond that was a reflection of her back. Past that was a reflection of her laying face up again.

Again.

And again.

And again.

Endlessly, she stared past herself. The repeating edges of the mirror stood like trees in the forest, one that stretched on into a hazy green mist that rolled and spread over the ground, reaching farther and farther. It shifted and moved like a crowd, marching endlessly.

Jackie stepped forward, tempted by the wonder before her. She stepped over the border of the mirror. Walking forward, Jackie shivered. The air was cold and with each step grew colder. A cloud of white blew out as she breathed, mixing into the thickening green mist.

Jackie's feet hit the ground. Her toes curled against the cold surface. It was like walking over ice. Each step brought her closer to the next mirror, and then the next and the next.

She walked, following a path to the unknown.

Unknown, yet unchanging.

Jackie knew nothing about where she was or where she would end up. She hardly noticed the wall of mirrors moving closer and closer. Each step carried her over another threshold. The green mist was growing thicker, swirling in cold waves around Jackie like beckoning arms. Her breath was lost in it.

A snap like thunder in the dead of night. Jackie's heart jumped. She blinked, taking in her surroundings.

She screamed. Her voice echoed back at her, again and again, spreading farther, but never vanishing. Jackie turned and ran the way she had come. The only thing before her was a reflection of what was now behind her. Each step took her through another mirror, each one as tall as the sky and stretched wider than what could be seen.

Jackie took a turn, running alongside the mirrors. Only a few steps and she was crossing a threshold, again and again. She stopped, stumbling on the smooth ground. She turned around, searching for anything that could help her.

She stood in a box, perfectly square. Beyond it, endless reflections of the same box. All the same. All empty, save for the mirror walls that made the green mist. Frozen, Jackie gaped as it swirled around her. An airy sound caught in her ears as shapes formed in the mist.

Shadows became faces. Empty eyes wide, staring blindly. Mouths pulled open as airy screams no louder than a faint whisper came from them. Agony and terror long lost danced around Jackie. They pushed against each other as if fighting for attention.

Everywhere Jackie turned, there were more and more of them. With nowhere else to look, her eyes searched upward. Above, far enough to be the sky, was a green-gray void. It sat so still and unchanging, it could be mistaken for a wall. A wall with a symbol.

No, a logo. One Jackie recognized.

Jackie fell to her knees as her world turned. The cold from the ground cut into her legs, making her nerves scream. The frost-filled air burned her lungs, suffocating her. Her body shook. With nowhere to go, Jackie ran.

The wailing mist followed her. Faces swirled around her, screaming silently. Jackie waved her arms, dispersing the green mist. As she sprinted onward, the faces became only thin wisps of fog. The wall beyond came closer and closer. The green tint was becoming brown as the mist pulled away like a curtain.

Walls slid around her, turning the endless space into a corridor. At the end: a wall the color of brown butcher paper. It stood over Jackie like a door over an ant. Around her was nothing but green, wailing mist. The blurred faces were becoming defined. Noses, hollow cheekbones, and black, sunken eyes dragged themselves toward her. Thin arms like skeletons were outstretched. She could feel something grabbing at her clothes.

Screaming, Jackie beat at the brown surface. It slid under her hands, shifting like a thin cover. She clawed at it, using her nails to tear at the material. It opened. Light poured from the holes. The voices hissed and faded as more and more light chased away the mist.

With a long rip, Jackie tore a hole large enough to push herself through. Half-blind, she was only able to take a few steps before colliding with something solid. Blinking the light from her eyes, she palmed at what blocked her path.

Glass.

What stood before her was an endless wall of glass.

Beyond it, she could see a shelf, though the distance between her and it was great. The shelf was large—as if she herself was the size of a mouse. Peering down, she could not see the floor below, but she could see that lining the shelf was a row of mirrors.

She recognized many of them from the shop—but this was impossible. She had to be dreaming.

A shadow passed over, and eyes the size of the sun stared down at her. A person. Giant, fitted for the world outside. A curious hand reached out, past where Jackie was trapped, and though her feet remained planted, the world beyond lurched forward.

The floor came up fast.

—

Ocean Blouth is an Austin, Texas resident, born and raised. Since early childhood they've had a passion for creating stories. With the benefit of being an avid daydreamer, they're rarely at a loss of writing ideas. Stretching across genres, their tales have a blend of cartoon logic and thriller consequences.

Surprise Otter

By Erynnis

Your first born was not what you expected. Being human, as your partner was, you never thought you'd give birth to an otter. It is said that surprises are good for the soul, my friend. It keeps you on your toes.

Your mother screeched at first, meeting her grandchild. It is also said, however, that a mother's love is unconditional.

Your pregnancy was peaceful, but now your mind is reeling with questions:

Will the nearby school be welcoming of their unusual student, when the time comes to get an education?

Does the grocery store carry otter-sized diapers?

However, you forget all of your concerns when your eyes meet those of the newborn child.

Instantly you know, from the swelling in your chest, that indeed the love of a mother knows no barriers.

—

Erynnis is a French woman living in Austin, TX. As her first writing project, she somehow thought that writing a seven book fantasy series in her second language was a good idea. She is a Reiki healer and Dungeon & Dragons game master. In her spare time, she can be found in the Barton Springs pool or hitting the nature trails.

Fiona at the Pool

By J.L. Zhang

Splashes erupted from a distance, chased by the sharp trill of a lifeguard's whistle. Fiona was ahead of me in the pool, her hair coiled into a large bun over her head as she stood there, looking at the other kids from a distance.

I gaped at her for a good moment before remembering my arms and legs could move, then carefully lowered myself down the pool stairs until the water hid my body. This was the scene of my attempted reinvention; seventh grade was around the corner in only a few short weeks. The last thing I wanted to be in was that ruffled pink monstrosity of a swimsuit my mother bought for me ages ago, but unfortunately that was what I wore that day.

"Cool swimsuit!" Fiona shouted and waved to me.

"Th-thanks..." I managed to reply, unsure of what to do with myself. Fiona gestured for me to come closer. I worked my way across the pool, keeping everything under my shoulder submerged.

Once I was within speaking distance, she grinned, displaying her set of rainbow-colored braces up close. "You also go to Bellham Middle, right? I'm Fiona."

"I'm So-Sophia," I croaked out, taken aback that she was actually speaking to me.

Fiona giggled. "My sister's also named Sophia! You know about her, right? She graduated this year. "

I nodded, not quite knowing how to respond.

"Well, anyways," she continued, "she's too cool to hang with me since getting into boarding school."

"Boarding school?" I repeated, wanting her to speak more.

"Yep!" Fiona slapped the surface of the water for extra effect. "A school where they smack your butt with boards! Get it? Boarding school?!" Some of the water landed on a group of older girls nearby, earning their scowls before they swam away from us.

I laughed, maybe a little harder than necessary. Fiona's sister was the school's swim star. I didn't know her, but, like everyone else, I knew of her.

We took laps together around the pool that afternoon, using the other swimmers as an obstacle course. Fiona went through every possible stroke there was to know with the mechanical diligence of someone who took paid lessons while I tried to keep up. Finally, after what felt like forever, she stopped. With relief, I held onto the side of the pool to catch my breath.

Fiona leaned over to speak. "Let's try..." She trailed off as though she was considering her options, then smirked as she nodded toward the lifeguard sitting under the shade. "Let's pull the shorts down on that guy."

Did my jaw drop?

Was it supposed to?

I dropped my jaw. "I don't think—"

"Oh puh-leeze!" Fiona rolled her eyes with an exasperated sigh. "Don't tell me you're too scared to have some fun."

I glanced at the lifeguard.

It was the eve of a new school year. I needed more friends. The inevitable was about to happen.

The pool was shaped like a four-pronged blob where, at strategic locations, it looked like you couldn't be seen above if you ducked your head low enough. We stalked the lifeguard—whom we decided should be named Fred—like a pair of crocodiles peering out over the edge of the water.

That day, Fred was one of three lifeguards who switched in and out of the pool office. The gossip over at the eight-feet side between some of the older middle school girls was that Fred was a college student back in his hometown for the summer.

We hid behind one of the tiled curves, away from a splash war that was now breaking out between a group of boys.

"What if we get caught?" I asked.

"We'll just have to make sure we don't get caught," Fiona replied.

"And how? People will see us doing it."

Fiona grinned. "Not if there's a distraction, they won't."

Peering out from his perch, Fred rarely left his chair except to take a break and switch places with one of the other lifeguards. The plan was to get him to leave his seat, but not go into the pool while everyone was distracted. According to Fiona, there was only one way to do this.

She left the pool momentarily. When she returned, she grabbed my hand and shoved something rough and hard into it.

I brought it up to take a closer look, "What—"

"*Shh*, don't!" Fiona hissed and slapped my hand back into the water before I could examine what it was. I glanced down at the small ridges peeking through my fingers near the surface of the water. A pinecone.

Fiona's eyes were wide with anticipation. "It's perfect, isn't it?" she whispered.

"What are we doing with this?" I asked, despite already knowing the answer.

"You're gonna let this float up in the pool, scream "poop," and everyone will turn to look," Fiona replied matter of factly.

"But they'll think I did it 'cause I'll be the closest to this thing!" I protested.

Fiona rolled her eyes, "No, they won't. Just go off to the side before yelling. C'mon, it'll be fun!"

Ahead of us was a group of girls too distracted by their gossip to notice my existence. I knew this was the moment I was going to follow through on something the old version of me never had the guts to do. Fiona gave me a smile and a thumbs up before turning and stepping out of the pool. Tightening my grip around that innocent pinecone, I crept as close as I could to them and willed myself to be invisible. Of all the times in my life, now was when I needed to be overlooked, disregarded, and completely forgettable. Then, taking a deep breath, I released the pinecone.

"POOP IN THE POOL! POOOOOP!!" I screamed and darted away as fast as possible from the crime scene.

Horrified and disgusted cries filled the air as everyone splashed their way out of the water in a frenzy. Fred immediately left his seat and walked to the edge of the pool. "Everyone get out!" he screamed into his speakerphone.

From the corner of my eyes, in the middle of the chaos, I could see Fiona creep up behind him. I held my breath.

In a flash, she tugged his swim shorts down.

I looked away as Fred f-bombed the entire community pool amidst laughter, rivaling my dad's profanity-laced tirades when his favorite football team lost. By the time I was brave enough to look again, Fred had already remedied his indecent exposure and the disaster was under control. Fiona, amazingly, slipped away without being seen.

One eagle-eyed parent spotted the suspicious-looking pinecone that we'd passed off as fecal matter. False alarm, everyone. After it became clear that no one was coming forward for shouting the poop alarm in the middle of the pool, people slowly trickled back into the water, perplexed at who was paranoid enough to scream over a pinecone.

The commotion gradually wore off and people returned to their mundane chatter. In the pool, I searched for the familiar head with a bun. A shape snuck up behind me, causing me to almost scream into a pair of hands that covered my mouth.

"Wasn't that fun?" Fiona giggled into my ear.

I turned around, a little irritated from being startled, but unable to suppress my grin. "I can't believe we pulled that off..."

Fiona laughed. "But we did it!" She stretched both of her arms above her dramatically and spun around in the water. Fred, who was red faced last I looked, had disappeared into the pool office, not to be seen again for the remaining hours of the pool's operation.

The light shifted as the sun started its descent from the sky. Adults were calling out the names of their children to go home. Glancing around us, most of the pool-goers had trickled out. The edge of the moon emerged, sunburnt from daylight that had finally begun to cede.

It was time. I turned to Fiona. "I need to tell you something," I began, but I stopped, because the simulation's expression didn't respond. For a split second, the reality peeked through.

With a deep breath, I took her hands into mine before everything ended. "I'm sorry I didn't say goodbye."

The image faded away and the sensation in my hands returned to what they were before, lightly clasped around two metal handles. Piercing cold air brushed against my head as the top portion of the capsule lifted up. I winced, adjusting to the light.

A young man, clothed in black, went around me to remove the last of the wirings and attachments as I sat quietly in the testing room. The consultant stood at a distance, preoccupied with notes she was typing in.

In reality, Fiona never got to pull down Fred's swim trunks. Her mother came and pulled her out of the pool in a fit of rage because she had snuck out of the house. That moment at the pool was the beginning of a ten-year friendship. It would end with me realizing that I was in love with her our senior year of college, and her explaining to me that she had started dating a mutual friend of ours.

"Did that go alright?" the consultant finally asked as she turned away from her screens and walked toward me. The young man retreated to the room next door as though that was his cue to leave.

"It was...okay," I replied, trying to figure out how many times I would have to go through the experience in order to finally have enough peace to sleep.

I had wanted to tell Fiona so many things. By the time she was getting married, I was halfway across the world trying to find myself, in an attempt to heal a broken heart that simply wouldn't mend. I was scared when her letter came, afraid to read about her happiness or deal with any possible attempt at a reconciliation. I was angry that my dad had given her my new address. Fiona's letter ended up sitting on my desk for weeks, then months, until I was finally able to open it one evening when I came back from the bars drunk after an outing.

Cancer. It was terminal.

I remember standing in my small studio, stunned. I never found the courage to respond, afraid to discover that I was too late. And now, twenty years later, there I was, spending my savings on this.

It was glitchy, but at least it resembled most of what I had in my head.

"We could, if you want, add even more to the experience," the consultant suggested as she took out her stylus and tablet for me to sign off.

For a second, I was tempted to take her up on the offer. If I were courageous enough, I would sell my house to pay for the scene where I come back to see the adult version of Fiona. But the adult version would only remind me of what I had failed at.

At least I was able to make sure that scene at the pool had perfect weather. It had actually been overcast that afternoon when I first became friends with Fiona.

"No," I replied. "This is...good for now."

I glanced up at the oversized monitor that displayed the last scene of my experience. Fiona stood in the middle of the pool, frozen on screen, looking up at a burnished moon far bigger than any she could've seen while alive.

Warlord

By Cooper Barham

Content warnings: Graphic imagery, genocide, racist/
classist/generally discriminatory behaviors

Note from the author:
This story exists as an experimental perspective shift on an undisclosed,
existing intellectual property, with the filing numbers shaved off, as it
were. Because of that, I recognize its content and manner of writing will
not be to everyone's liking. I wrote it in such a way that I believe it could
still be enjoyable, but I acknowledge certain audiences that identify the
source material and POV character are likely to understand and
appreciate it more than others.
For this, I only partially apologize. This writing approach may not be
convenient for everyone, but it's a story I deeply enjoyed writing, and
which has no opportunity to be published elsewhere. Forgive me this
indulgence, and enjoy!

—

You were born on an ordinary day in an extraordinary universe.

You didn't know it then, but you were reared into the darkest folds of nepotism. A space warlord by birth, you were acquainted with a life of slaves, servants, and soldiers, long before you could understand the implications of such things. These were gifts from your family, whose bloodline possessed an unfair bounty of inherent power. They deemed this reason enough to subjugate others in whatever way suited their liking, and you took to this policy naturally.

As a young warlord, you would claim your first kill at the age of three. As a child practices how to move their body, so did you practice what your own body was capable of. One day, a couple of friendly neurotransmitters connected in your brain, and you knew with the ease of breathing how to craft semi-material energy in the palm of your hand. It sort of came out, all soft light and colorful warmth. The energy was pure and held a rosy pink tint.

What was this? It was almost like imagination, manifest. You were excited by your self-discovery, something you'd found all on your own. You were eager to show your handler, but being untrained as you were, you accidentally let the energy stray from your grasp.

It traveled quickly, like a star streaking through the sky. It punctured your handler's armor (for everyone in your family's service wore armor at all hours, as a matter of military readiness), and passed through, exploding against the far hull of the interstellar ship you called home.

You witnessed this development, astonished. You were not horrified, but curious, and immediately set about how you might do it again.

When your family found what you'd done, they were not upset at the casualty, but proud of your growth. They lifted you up. Praised you. Volunteered a new handler as replacement.

You were far too young to know, but even from such a young age, the seeds of your sadism had begun to germinate. Before long, the universe would learn to fear the young warlord, and your name would be synonymous with terror itself.

By the time you were six years old, you'd already killed your mother. The only surprising thing about it was that your elder brother, just as selfish and nearly as cruel, had not done so already.

It was so simple. You pointed like the finger of God—*let there be light*—and the next, her heart was spilling a violet ichor onto the floor, like melted candy. A single perfect hole through her chest. She was gone within moments, and you thought maybe you saw pride in her eyes as she died. Hmm.

Your father was furious of course, though not as furious as another father might have been. It was no trivial loss, but ah, the promise. The ease of your destruction showed such promise for your future, as one destined to colonize the universe. To crush the throats of the defiant, to pull apart worlds and landscapes and civilizations—all nothing more than toys before you. Fools, filth, trash.

Not that your family *wanted* to destroy everything. Wanton destruction had diminishing returns. But it was good to know you *could* impose yourself upon the lesser species whenever the situation—or your whims—deemed it appropriate.

The green people would learn this the hard way, when they tried to hide something precious from you. But oh, we're getting ahead of ourselves, young warlord. That is not for years to come, and much blood will be shed in the meantime.

Adolescence emerged within you like the creation of time and space, heralding with it a ghastly, godless force. You could feel it in how you moved, how your body eluded any external pain that wasn't dealt by your father or brother—the only few with power comparable to yours. As you filled out, you began to look more like them—skin smooth and hairless, the bones of your feet stretching into a trident of digits for optimal balance. Growing your first tail was a miserable experience, as it was for all of your kind. Growing new vertebrae is hard work.

You did not have your brother's height, nor your father's horns, and that was all the better. Fools wouldn't help but underestimate you.

In all the universe and its endless stars upon stars, you hadn't met even one warrior who could hurt you. Not a single weapon that so much as broke the surface of your skin. When you descended upon them to enslave and control—no need to mince words, your actions were not kind, as kindness was what the weak chose to value when they had no strength to do as they pleased—they would inevitably assail you with their mightiest offerings, champions forged with lifetimes of battle. It was admirable, really, how they set aside all their civil differences to unite against your family. That was the depth of their fear.

As well it should be.

No matter their ferocity relative to their own kind, all of those champions fell, always without the tracest effort on your behalf. When you desired, they were unable to so much as touch you, their attacks and missiles chasing images of you, their minds unable to fathom or adequately process how quickly you could move. When you didn't care to evade, they would strike with all their force, knuckles breaking upon impact with the parts of your body that they assumed must be vulnerable—your nose, your eyes, your throat.

When you killed them, you were either blindingly efficient, striking down dozens in a matter of seconds, or you took your time, slowly twisting limbs apart with your bare hands and crushing their skulls with great deliberation, savoring the squelch of their brains as they leaked out between your fingers.

You fancied yourself a god. You were more often decried as a devil.

Both made you feel warm inside.

Of course, we cannot record this story without a mention of the monkeys, damnable as they could be. I know of your hate, but you understand, don't you? It's a matter of posterity, young warlord.

You feared nobody, this much has been made evident. But you know the truth as well as I: this doesn't mean you feared nothing. You feared the monkeys, that bestial race of men on their caustic, war-ruined world. You feared them not for the threat they presented, but the potential you saw in them to grow, to flourish, to surpass. They were in your employ, your most useful soldiers. Your family leashed them, but allowed that leash to travel far, so they could sate the bloodlust and craving for violence that ran through their blood. Because they were yours, you witnessed their growth first-hand, and the uncanny way their power multiplied with time. Still utterly dwarfed by yours, of course, but exponentially above all others.

Most of all, you feared a myth. An echo of their lore, a fraction of mythology, orally guided through the generations, suggesting that there was once a monkey of such enormity that his power could be likened only to...well, to you. Absurd, of course. Preposterous. Hideous and laughable to even think it.

A stupid monkey legend. A folktale to placate them, and provide hope to their stupid monkey children.

But still, when alone in your room trying to sleep, your imaginings betrayed you, and you wondered darkly.

So you watched the monkey species closely. In time, you assassinated their king and took his son as your subject and trophy, so not even the best among them dare challenge you.

Until they did. One of those damn, putrid apes, drunk on his own confidence, emerged from the stinking riff raff of his kind, in an indignant fury that sought to strike you down. See, this is what you'd warned father and brother about. You told them the monkeys would rise up. The pride in their blood boiled too greatly to be shackled, the hate and violence writhed in their souls, demanding they kill. The monkeys were a warrior race, after all. They would rather die than embrace servitude.

Such was a fate easily accommodated. So, you alone would bring down their armies. A single, galactic nova of power, at the tip of your finger, sent crashing into their world, lighting it up like a planetary candle, smelting it into glass and slag and exposing the bright, molten wound of its core.

Of course, you ensured that in your, ah, genocidal contingency, the death of the foolhardy one who rose up against you was first to die, disintegrated beyond bone and sinew, his molecules scattered into the universe with the soundless blast of his home planet ripping apart. That little rose-colored energy you made as a child, now casually wiping out all resistance from the most prideful, most troublesome race in the boundless cosmos.

Nobody else was there to remember, young warlord, the way you laughed. But I remember.

I remember the joy and relief it brought you, as you turned a billion souls into solar ash.

Twenty years would go by, and you'd remain eternally uncontested. No longer a young warlord, but a true, deific onslaught whose name made a hundred thousand galaxies shudder. Now just the fearsome, invincible harbinger of death that your father always saw in you. A child who could vaporize solar systems.

Sometimes you'd think about your mother. How pathetic she was. She deserved to die, if she was weak enough to be killed by a child. That stupid, weak woman. You would never allow such a thing, if you were in her place.

They were all gone, now. Your father was off chasing new galactic enterprises, expanding your family's trade empire. Your brother was left to survey and maintain his own quadrant of the universe, like yourself. You had eight-hundred and eighty-eight thousand worlds, hundreds of trillions of lives under your jurisdiction. You possessed an army billions strong, pulled from the strongest soldiers of the strongest planets and equipped with the most prodigious technology the smartest military scientists had to offer.

The monkey prince was grown now, and served you faithfully, if not enthusiastically. You knew he hated you, but what did it matter? He was alone, the most powerful of his kind, and not even close enough to breathe on the bottomless chasm of your strength. You kept him around now because he was a novelty—a useful trinket. His pride was immense, and you enjoyed teasing him with the futility of it all.

One day the little shit would try to kill you, obviously, and you'd finally grant his wish to die. Swiftly, just like you'd killed his father.

Those days were long, and your greatest enemy was no army or warrior. Not even the fear of a dead monkey legend. Now your only threats were boredom and a running clock. You lost sleep over your mortality, that fragile, obscene truth. You were in no danger of sudden death or assassination, and the rare attempts to slay you with poison proved futile. Your only threat was time, and the inevitable weakness of age.

Then, one day, almost by accident, you'd learn of another legend. A planet full of green people, lingering just barely outside your known influence. They had supernatural artifacts local to their little world, which when collected together, could summon forth an all-powerful dragon, or so it goes—a dragon that could grant any wish you asked of it.

Suddenly, dear warlord, you had a convenient solution to your boredom and mortality. A fun hunt, as it were. How'd that saying go, on the monkey world? Ah yes, "something to kill the time."

For were you truly a god, if you could not defy the imminence of time itself?

No. Not yet.

But it was inevitable.

On the other side of the universe, while the warlord grew into his destiny, there was another figure of great importance: a young boy who deserves a moment of our attention. Yes, this story is not about one, but two.

He who would be warlord, and the second: a cheerful, oafish young man who liked to eat fish.

Listen close, dear reader, for this part is a secret I carry to you. The warlord cannot see these words. That is one of his weaknesses, you know. So much power, yet such limited vision. But this part is just for you and I, and so I am confiding in you this hidden truth:

The warlord made a mistake.

The warlord, born into the demonic salvation of his bloodline, had thrown around a power that he inherited from birth. A monster so sick and so vast that his existence had to be a cosmic joke.

And yet, as he enacted untold violence across the infinite stars, carving his legacy in blood and screams, a young boy grew up in peace, on a planet far from the warlord's reach.

This young boy knew he was different from those around him, but for a long time wouldn't know how, or why. His story is a long one, told elsewhere, but there's a few things you need to hear, to understand why I include him in this recollection.

Most importantly, he was innocent: a visage of kindness and representative of hope. Any anger he wielded, he did so honorably, in defense of others. He loved combat, it was in his blood, but he evaded carnage. It was within his power to slaughter indiscriminately, but he chased friendly competition, protected the weak, and sought in all things to constantly improve himself.

He made friends not by trying, but through the sheer, addictive force of his goodness. He was light, he was gravity.

And my friend, I cannot express to you the joy that brings me. Because I have withheld the most important detail: he was, if you can believe it, a child of the monkeys, spared the obliteration of his race through mere, cosmic accident.

In his infancy he was sent to enslave the people of his world, to requisition them for the warlord's eventual domination. But as fate would have it, he'd sustain a head injury that would banish his innate impulse to destroy, and he'd be raised among snowy, quiet mountains by an old man who'd never had a son of his own. The young boy was reared to embody mercy, cherish self-discipline, and cultivate the strength that others deserved.

Instead of subjugation, he would become the hero of that world. A young man—a monkey—easily recognized by the clothing on his back: the signature orange fatigues of the masters who helped him master himself.

And when, as a gesture of divine hilarity, the monkey prince would lay siege upon this young man's world, the only one who could ever hope to resist him was, of course, the monkey in orange. Both of them the last of their kind: one was the warlord's greatest asset, the other a discarded child, so insignificant as to be forgotten or assumed dead when he failed to complete his mission. A warrior elite versus a low-born, common monkey peasant, reared on compassion and gentleness.

It would become a shame that haunted the monkey prince for the rest of his life, the day that common soldier defeated him in battle. The monkey prince did all in his power to claim victory, even threatening destruction of the monkey in orange's home planet, vanquishing it the same way the warlord had to his own.

But it wasn't enough, and the monkey prince dragged himself broken and defeated to the ship he'd arrived in, the wounds of that loss cutting valleys into his pride, made all the worse because the monkey in orange *spared* him. He'd been shown *mercy*, a foreign concept in the monkey prince's reality. The warlord had never shown anyone mercy.

It was the gravest of insults, and the monkey prince carved a promise of retribution into his heart, that he would seek out the monkey in orange and take his revenge.

But that is not how fate was designed.

A year later, much will have changed, you see.

It is here our narratives converge.

Remember, this is a secret, so though I am about to leave you, take these last words of mine and hold them close. They are too important to let stray, and the warlord can never know:

That young boy, the monkey in orange, was the hope of the universe.

Yes, dear warlord, I am still here. My attention is entirely and eternally yours. My family lives and dies for you. Where were we?

Of course. The green people, as you call them.

Oh warlord, see how predictable they are? They run, they hide, they fight, though they know they cannot escape or challenge you. You are a miracle of physical permanence and absolute authority. If one of them made you bleed a little, you would be delighted! For none anywhere, ever, had succeeded in doing so. Besides your asshole brother, of course, and the sharp physical reprimands of your father.

Bleeding would be a novelty.

It would give you reason to try.

To give a shit.

But no, they could not. You'd already surpassed this world's greatest offerings by the time you were six years old. Best to find the artifacts you sought, summon this so-called "almighty dragon," of theirs, wish for immortal youth, and be done with it. Then you would truly have nothing left to fear. Not even the laws of reality.

You would be above reality.

Maybe you'd kill your brother. He *was* an asshole. Hmm, something to consider.

Ah, but it wouldn't be so simple, retrieving the artifacts needed to make your wish. The monkey prince was there, on the green people planet! And it seems he'd finally decided to challenge you! Of course, being the monkey that he was, he had no creativity of his own, and wanted only what you want: to live forever in strength. Monkey see, monkey do, haha.

And he did complicate things a bit, sure. Him and a couple others who didn't belong on this planet. Allies of his, it seemed. A couple of short...ah, you'd seen this race before, hadn't you? Humans, if you recall? Another type of monkey, from another solar system. What was the monkey prince doing with a couple of humans?

No matter. Your campaign to collect the artifacts was inevitable, as you were inevitable, and before long, you were standing before your prize, prepared to wish for life, eternal.

Except the legend had rules, and you weren't paying close enough attention. You did not know there was an ancient green person, suffering all the years of age and weakness of mortality—the exact thing you'd wished to avoid. You did not know that when this green elder died, the power of the artifacts died with him.

You did not know this, when you killed him.

~~You inane piece of shit.~~

Oh, how you raged, dear warlord. How your heart was so filled with hatred for all things that you considered, for a moment, the indiscriminate annihilation of all things. To hell and damnation with your family's empire. You'd leave an intergalactic inferno in the wake of your anger. How unjust the universe must be, to deny you this one thing that you wanted most of all!

You were right, though not how you meant. This was not a just universe. ~~A just universe would never tolerate someone like you.~~

I'm finding myself distracted, my lord. Apologies. It won't happen again.

As for the monkey prince and the humans who tagged along beside him: they caught you in the midst of your fury, as black as space is dark. You saw them, and you knew, you would kill these first of all, before genociding the rest of reality. If you were to die, it would come only after all else had been wiped away! At this point, it was unlikely even your family could stop you.

But when the monkey prince attacked you, it—well, it didn't hurt, but the force of it was surprising. He had become so strong. So many battles had the monkey prince endured that the advantage of his blood had transformed him into something greater.

It was with peerless audacity that he claimed to be the living legend you'd feared for so long. The first in a thousand years. The ultimate being, above all others.

Like hell he was. You'd torture him, before he died. You'd promised to kill him swiftly, but no. Your soul, formless and boiling over with cruelty, demanded that you hurt something. Not simply destroy, but cause anguish, grief, misery, pain, suffering, agony.

The monkey prince's efforts were trivial, and the humans' even less. By the time you were done, the stupid, foul-brained monkey prince lay on the ground, his pride crippled to reflect his back as you broke it in half.

Blood leaked out from so many wounds, his fingers wrenched into unsightly shapes, one eye blinded. He couldn't move, could barely even speak. You were surprised he was even conscious, but after all, he was very stubborn. Such was the nature of those apes.

Then something happened. Once again, your expectations were turned sideways, for there was not one, but two full-blooded monkeys left. As the prince fell, another had joined their motley crew of weaklings, this one donning fatigues of a garish orange, and his face...

Something about this one made you hate him more than the rest. He looked so...familiar? Why was that?

Why did it seem that the prince and the monkey in orange knew each other? How and when could such a thing have happened? Kinship through shared blood, maybe?

The prince dispensed his final words through the most pathetic tearful goodbye you'd ever seen. You would have never imagined he was capable of such a disgraceful end. His pride, it seemed, held no value after all.

It hurt him so mightily to speak, and yet he pushed through. It was important he tell the monkey in orange that you, dear warlord, were responsible for the extinction of their race, their home planet. How you forced them all into slavery before you killed them. How you cut down the prince's father before his eyes, and forced him into indentured servitude as a child.

The prince went so far as to claim that he was himself a monster. And he was a monster because of you. That you'd *made* him that way. That was rich.

You lifted a single finger, and cut him off mid-sentence with a beam of light through his heart.

The finger of god. Killer of worlds. Killer of kings and would-be's.

The monkey prince breathed his last.

So we've reached the present, dear warlord. Here, on an unbecoming, backwater planet, where only you and a few others remain, the rest butchered in your casual disregard for life. Your trophy, the monkey prince, has stopped moving.

That left just one monkey remaining, the new one. You'll end him too, but dammit, why did his face bother you so?

It is time to finish what you started. Time to kill the last of the m—

Suddenly, you are dazed, your sense of space divided into halves. Pain blooms in your nose. What the—

A force crashes into your stomach, driving the wind out of your lungs. Spittle flings from your lips.

It takes only a moment for you to recover, to create distance and restore order, but for a moment, the monkey in orange—the last monkey—he...he *hurt* you?

None had succeeded. Not a single soul outside your bloodline had ever—

You feel a slight trickle of blood leave your left nostril and wipe it away immediately. You chuckle wryly. Oh, interesting. How *fun*.

Then the fight begins in earnest.

The last monkey, he—he's stronger than you could have ever imagined. Certainly if he wanted, he could also be a destroyer of worlds. A *mere monkey* was trading blows with you, the most powerful being in the universe!

With every strike one of you lands on the other, the world distorts, breaking beneath the magnitude of your combat. You move so quickly that sound itself cannot keep up and the land turns to a golden slag with your passing. Every attack sends thunder that ripples and bends the planet's atmosphere. Wounds open in the earth, and volcanic blood spills into the sky.

It quickly becomes clear that in spite of this unbelievable development, you still reign supreme. The last monkey is eons beyond his contemporaries, but you, you remain above him. As he grows exhausted, you finally break a sweat. Well played, good monkey!

But still, he persists. He cries about how he will vanquish you at all costs, and he's impressed you so much that you can't help but laugh.

He has to die, of course. No one must ever see what he's done. No soul must ever know you are still mortal.

The last monkey has some fun tricks, some creative gimmicks, and to his credit, lands several very painful strikes upon your body, breaking open your flesh and rocking your skull. But none of it is enough.

What *is* nearly enough is his final gambit. As his friends distract you, he collects energy far above, in the vacuum of space, where you can't see it.

By the time you know their plot, a globe of radiant blue is descending upon you, itself so large that it consumes your entire line of sight. You dare not evade it, of course. You cannot show that you are afraid of how much damage it could do. It is nothing.

So you grab it, even as it drives you down into the earth. You've never felt something so heavy, so unstoppable. What is this? How is it possible for something to exist that you cannot stop? You are immutable.

Your body is drowned in light and power, scalding your flesh and exploding with force.

For a moment, you believe in your heart of hearts that you've made a mistake. You believe you have died.

You find them celebrating your defeat ten minutes later, when you erect yourself from the city-sized wound their assault made on the green people's planet.

There's no room left in you for curiosity, or amusement, or sport, as you shrug off the debris and humiliation.

Nobody has ever hurt you like this.

Nobody.

Not one fucking weakling loser in this entire damned cosmos. Not even your brother and father. They never tried to *kill* you, and you doubt that with your strength, they would ever even try.

You lift your finger, and kill one of the humans. Bang. Gone in a flash of light, utterly deleted.

There. That's right. That's how it should be. Everything fucking dies before you.

You are a destroyer of worlds. You will kill the entire motherfucking universe before you let these ants, these *atoms* make a fool of you!

The weather starts to turn.

You notice a chill in the air as you take aim at the other human, this one a child. You're going to kill him next.

A shiver like death rattles your body, giving you pause.

The last monkey, he's...something was happening. He's hunched, shoulders heaving like the ceiling of a cage, barely containing an unseen animal trapped inside. In his expression, where you expected to see hopelessness and defeat, you see something else: the whites of teeth bared, as if to rip apart meat. The muscles of his face tighten and shift with spasms of wrath, as if his very soul was ripping off a mask, revealing something else within.

"*I won't let you get away with this,*" his voice is strained, like a cord of metal pulled too thin.

The sea around you begins to boil. The sky spins together with the shadows of storms, blades of lightning cutting through the horizon. Land splits and fragments lift upwards towards the heavens, as if the monkey's anger was enough to reengineer gravity itself.

It doesn't even occur to you to shoot him and stop whatever is happening from happening.

The last monkey's body is convulsing with controlled rage. You could see the vengeance sharpening in his eyes and realize with dawning horror that until this moment, he was fighting you out of a moral imperative. He was a man who considered himself good, just doing right by those around him. That man, for all his ferocity, didn't want to kill you.

But now something else was emerging in his place.

Oh. That's how you knew him. Now that there is hatred inside his eyes, you can see it so clearly. The way he wants to hurt you, it's just like that monkey who rebelled decades ago, the one who prompted you to act, to finally immolate the monkey planet.

No. It couldn't be. Was that fool this monkey's fath—

The last monkey screamed, and with it came a radiant fury of light.

When you were young, you saw an artistic rendering of the monkey legend, the supposed beast-man with the power to crush gods. You saw it and laughed, because it was huge, brutish, and primal. Absolutely ridiculous. Such an easy, slow, stupid target.

The truth was so much simpler.

A man with golden hair glares at you and you know his disdain is explicitly personal. The last monkey has changed in such a way that, despite having never seen it before, you know in the shadows of your heart that this is what you always feared. This was their thousand-year-old legend, born anew.

It could be nothing else.

He asked the human child to leave, patiently once, and then with an animal roar the next.

You aren't sure what to do. You aren't sure what's happening. You take aim to shoot the boy. No witnesses.

You're surprised when the golden monkey is suddenly standing in front of you. You're surprised when he grabs your hand.

You're surprised how much it hurts when he slowly tightens his grip, crushing your knuckles together a little more each second. You're surprised, and desperate, when you can't seem to free yourself.

Until he lets you go.

There's a coldness now, in those eyes. A gentleness, slaughtered.

"That was my best friend," he says with a resigned sadness. "How many billions of innocent people have died at your hands? When will it be enough? Did you have *fun*?"

You don't answer. You don't lower yourself to the level of a fat, stupid ape. You needn't justify yourself to him.

You attack.

Trying to hit him is a disorienting charade, like trying to strike a ghost. He moves in such quick, slight ways that you second-guess whether he dodged, or you simply missed.

This infuriates you, and you curse him and his name. You damn him to hell, promise to put him in the ground and spit on the grave, if only you could hit him.

The golden monkey does not smile, does not move, does not say anything. He only waits, and watches.

You lift the finger of god. A rosy pink glint forms at the tip and you point it directly at his forehead.

Bang.

A beam as fast as light itself. A time-tested promise of blood. The inevitable end of all things.

You watch as the golden monkey's head snaps back with the impact, and—

But that's not what's supposed to happen. The sound it made...was that of something bouncing off a surface.

You did not know the beam *could* make a sound.

The golden monkey slowly returns to position, a very slight scuff on his forehead.

How was this possible?

You are a killer of kings. There are ten thousand religions that worship you as an almighty permanence. You butcher those that others would call gods. Legions of widows and orphans weep across the cosmos where you've tread.

Where you point, things die.

"Is that it?"

Those are the last words the golden monkey says before he beats the shit out of you.

With every punch to the gut, the world shakes a little.

Every elbow to the jaw scatters the clouds.

When he kicks you to the earth, the land collapses into the sea.

This cannot be happening.

There is an immutable declaration within the foundations of reality, one that decrees you as the sole proprietor of all authority. All living beings are mere playthings to you. Nobody can comprehend your power and cunning.

So why is it that the harder you struggle, the more futile it seems?

The more you push yourself to move a little faster, to hit a little harder, the further out of reach victory becomes.

You can feel your ribs cracking. Your teeth feel loose and blood leaks out from the gums.

Fuck. Fuck, fuck, fuck!

Even at your fullest power, it's all you can do just to keep up with the golden monkey. But despite all your effort, you can't help but feel he's toying with you. A cat tossing around a mouse until it dies of exhaustion.

Why—

Why was it like this?

How cruel and obscene could the universe be—how traitorous—to allow you to come so close to immortality, only to steal it out from beneath you, and replace it with—

A kick nearly breaks your neck. Instead it just sends you careening into a mountain. You immediately retaliate and he counters with another kick in your ribs, folding you in half and concussing you with a headbutt to the skull.

Your divine birthright is slipping out from between your fingers. Your dreams of ruling the entire universe forever, as its one, true god above all. Reduced to ashes by a filthy, braindead ape.

No!

A strike to your solar plexus. A heel to your knee.

No, no!

An elbow that knocks free a tooth, gushing blood across your tongue.

No, no, no!

A jab to your throat, several more to your gut, in quick succession.

No no no no no no no no—

Why. Couldn't. You. Hurt. *Him*?

But there was no answer. You just couldn't. He was simply better than you.

A devastating blow to your stomach causes something to burst inside, expelling toxins into your body. You fall to your knees, shaking as the pain arcs in circles around your nervous system. Your vision is blind with tears, unwillingly shed.

He is beside you, waiting.

"Stand up," he says. "Die on your feet."

No...you can't die. You are infinite! Absolute! And...

He leans over, curls his fingers around your throat, and lifts you until you're standing.

And...and...

Forgive me for smiling as I record this part. I've waited so long.

Do you see now, dear warlord? Do you see what I stood to gain from recording this chronicle?

For what better story is there in all of time and space, than the fall of history's greatest loser?

It almost makes up for watching you kill the ones I loved. Was their peerless subservience not enough? Do you even remember their faces?

Don't be petulant now. Don't cry like the monkey prince did. Not after how you condemned him for it. You? *A hypocrite?* Never.

It's funny, I think. The irony. The very, very last monkey is the one who would be your end. The only people you ever feared. You were so close, hahaha.

It's delicious watching you squirm and whine and plead and bitch about how unfair the universe is. You don't even hear what you're saying, do you?

You should be embarrassed and ashamed.

I'm glad I had the opportunity to share this moment with you. It was a long time coming, watching someone escort you into hell.

But we haven't even reached my favorite part yet.

Wait for it.

You make one final, awkward, limping maneuver to take off the golden monkey's head. He slips beneath your swing, desperate and clunky.

He steps forward in force, and punches a hole clear through your septic, black heart.

It doesn't even hurt. You just feel...absence.

Ah, so that's how it felt when you killed your mother.

At long last, with his battle at its end, the golden monkey leaves you to die, believing you are already gone. But you and I know the truth. You're still in there somewhere, clinging on to the last dredges of life, praying to gods you destroyed. It's sad, really. You are going to die here, alone, on a planet whose name you can't remember, slain by a monkey whose name you never bothered to learn.

Good. I am glad.

May time forget you, as you deserve. May all the universe finally heal, and all the pain you caused be reduced to a distant memory. We are owed that much.

Be forgotten, and inherit the end befitting of all warlords.

Manifesto for Platonic Touch

By Erynnis

You need to be touched.

That's just being human.

Normalize touching your friends when you speak.

Rest your head on their shoulder while watching a touching movie.

Grab their arm when you get scared or excited.
Give massages as an act of service
Hold hands

Normalize kisses as a form of platonic affection.

Snuggle with your friends.

Wrestle for fun. Engage in pillow fights. Build blanket forts and create a snuggle pit.

Hang out as friends and develop your emotional intimacy to feed
physical intimacy.
Keep your hands above the chest and below the thigh.
As always, your intention is the key.

Not all physical interaction has to lead to sex.
We need 12 hugs a day for growth.
Are you getting enough?

Real Cracker White Trash

By John W. Treviño

Content warnings: verbal abuse, attempted assault

Bastard's was a tourist spot in Daytona Beach. It was tacky and typical, with ugly decor and an entire side open, facing the sea, so that tourists could walk up off the sand and onto the concrete floor, buy a beer from the bar, and wander back out. It was raining, and the wind blew a fine mist of rain around John and Susan's legs. They sat together at the bar, which looped through the center of Bastard's in an O, dominating the space.

The waitress and the bartender talked quietly at the other end of the O, keeping an eye on John and Susan. There were no other customers. Susan had her phone up against her ear, waiting for someone to answer. After a moment, the ringing stopped and a man's voice came through, loud enough for John to hear it. Voicemail. She hung up.

"Still no answer?" John asked.

"Do you see me talking to anyone?" She frowned. "He'll be here."

"I'm sure," John said. "he'll have some sort of story."

Susan rolled her eyes. "Just stop." She grabbed her purse. "I'm going to the bathroom. I'll be a minute."

She stalked away.

John sighed, put his head in his hands, and closed his eyes.

"She's mad," John opened his eyes to see the waitress leaning against the bar next to him. The waitress: white shorts, a Bastard's tank top, pink push-up bra, dyed blonde hair stressed by too tight a perm, and skin aged by the sun. Age unknown. She smiled, pink lipstick smeared on teeth.

"My girlfriend," John said. "We're waiting for this guy. It's the last day of our vacation and we're just sitting around."

The waitress looked at the rain outside. "You're stuck with us right now anyway."

John shook his head. "He's always late. I'm bored."

The waitress set the bill on the bar, next to John, but instead of walking away she took Susan's stool. "He's not your friend."

John shook his head.

"He does this a lot?" she asked.

He nodded. "He always has an excuse."

"What's his best one?" the waitress asked.

John considered it. "He was coming to a dinner Suzie was having—"

"Your girlfriend?"

"Yeah," John said. "He was an hour late. He said that the side he'd made had too much garlic and he didn't want to stink up his car, so he made a different one."

The waitress laughed. "I haven't heard that one before."

"It's so stupid," he said. "I'm John, by the way."

"Cammy," she said, holding out a hand to shake.

"What's the best excuse you've heard?" John asked.

"Alligators ate his dog," Cammy said. Off John's horrified look: "oh no, the dog was fine! He just thought that sympathy and some smart waterworks would get him laid."

"How'd that go?" John asked.

Cammy cocked an eyebrow and fixed him with a look. "That's your one, Mr. John. I may be real cracker white trash, but I'm not that kind of girl. Or maybe I am. But you can't treat me like I am."

John held up his hands. "My bad, that wasn't fair."

She settled back in. "That's okay."

She slid her hand off of his knee, running it down the inside of his thigh before putting it back in her lap.

"I'd be happy if he were eaten by gators."

"It's a good excuse," Cammy said. She swiveled around facing him. Her legs touched his. "But you know what I think would be better? A sinkhole. Florida's got a ton of them. He could go General Lee. Boop! Straight in."

"You know what would be even better?" John said. "If he went into a sinkhole full of alligators."

"There you go!" She wrinkled her brow. "But, you know, this is Florida. We've got a bunch more hazards, like serial killers or Florida Man."

Susan walked out of the bathroom. Cammy swiveled away, her legs no longer against John's. She moved her hand off of her lap, though, and surreptitiously set it on his thigh. Susan walked over to the bartender, started to talk.

"We should stop there," John said.

"We shouldn't stop there!" Cammy said, warming up. "There's the Florida Skunk Ape!" She bared her teeth and mimed tearing with claws. "He's like our Bigfoot. He's supposed to stink really bad, too! Maybe Tim's airing out his car right now."

"Or it ate him," John said.

Cammy ran a finger up and down John's thigh. "That's good too."

John looked over at Susan, who was talking to the bartender, but watching them. He smiled at her. Cammy smiled and waved before turning back to John. He took his hand off of the bar, ran a finger along Cammy's thigh.

"So," John went on, "anymore urban legends that can eat Suzie's friend?"

Cammy looked over at Susan, who was still talking to the bartender, but watching Cammy. John could tell that something wasn't sitting right with Susan. He smiled at her. Susan, sour, begrudgingly turned her attention back to the bartender. John knew he was in for it with her no matter what he did next. John took his hand off of the bar, ran a finger along Cammy's thigh.

Cammy leaned towards him, kinky hair falling forward. "Well, the one that fucks me up was the Cassadaga Children."

John watched Susan. She had her purse on the bar and was fishing around inside. Aha, she wanted a pen. John turned his attention back to Cammy. "What?"

"Cassadaga! Where do you live?"

"Winter Park," he said. A glance across the bar: Susan writing something down on a slip of receipt paper.

"So you'll pass by on your way home! Cassadaga claims it's the most psychic place in the world."

John rolled his eyes, but Cammy went on: "No no! See, back in the day there was this witch who befriended all of the children there. She supposedly killed all of the town's children, but she cast a spell on the townsfolk and they couldn't stop her."

Susan nodded at something the bartender said and picked up her purse. Cammy and John pulled away from one another just as Susan approached the meet cute.

"Suzie, this is Cammy," John said.

"Oh!" Cammy said, reaching across John to grab Susan's hand. "Susan, I like your nails."

"She started getting them done when Tim told her he liked manicures," John said.

Susan pulled her hand away and said to Cammy, "John doesn't like Tim, because Tim and I used to date."

Cammy served John a sidelong look with a smile. "You're the jealous type?" Cammy looked up at Susan. "You should hear about all my boyfriends!"

John said, "You're leaving out, Suzie, that he still loves you."

"I give up," Susan said. "Let's go. The rain stopped. I told the bartender that if Tim shows, we've gone. I don't know why he's not answering his phone."

Susan fished cash out of her purse, tossed it onto the bill, and stormed off.

John ran after Susan. As he stepped onto the beach he looked back at Cammy, still at the bar. She blew him a kiss.

Back on the highway, they drove on in silence. Susan leaned her head against the window and stared at the pine forest passing by. John kept his eyes on the road.

In the distance, along the shoulder, a small, blue dot. As they neared it took shape.

"Look," John said, pointing. "A hitchhiker."

Susan could not care less. "Don't pick him up."

"But it could be Tim!"

Susan turned in her seat to get a better look at him. John could only spare her a glance, but her withering look was enough.

"I'm just having fun, Susan."

"We've just had a fight about Tim," Susan said. "Right now I'm too raw to find it funny."

He scowled.

They rocketed past the hitchhiker, a bum in the traditional definition, with a camping backpack, a bedroll, and walking sticks.

"Give me some time," Susan said. "I need to sort myself out. Maybe I'm just overreacting."

John shut up and drove on. She couldn't quite put her finger on what happened, John knew, and he wasn't about to clear things up. As they drove on, he thought about Cammy and realized that Susan's insecurity could work in his favor. He would like to hear all about

Cammy's boyfriends. That's different. He didn't need to be jealous with Cammy.

He worked through the different outcomes of a breakup and he settled on the one he thought suited him best. If Suzie dumped him, she wouldn't be able to pin it down to anything he did: it was just her suspicions getting to her. It would look paranoid to their friends. He convinced himself that Tim would make a beeline for Susan. In her emotional weakness she might even take him back. John would put out there that he always worried Susan was cheating. That would seal it for their friends: Susan sabotaged her relationship *and* Tim's. John was the good guy, Susan an untrustworthy whore. He would win the breakup, keep the friends, and see Susan and Tim cast out. He wouldn't have to deal with them anymore.

But all of his scenarios featured Cammy. He'd have to keep her hidden until Susan was well and truly gone. Cammy seemed too brash to be in the background for that long, but maybe? His friends might not like Cammy anyway: she was of a type you only find in Florida and the Gulf Coast east of the Mississippi. He'd put money that she smoked off work, didn't even consider going to college, and thought that stripping was a real job. There might even be a kid somewhere in there. Real Cracker White Trash. Maybe she wasn't a great long term option, then. But she could be short term. He was pretty sure she was used to that.

A billboard caught John's eye. "Cassadaga: Psychic Capital of the World!" He pointed and said to Susan: "Hey! That's the town Cammy was talking about."

"Yeah."

"I want to see it," John said.

"John, please. Let's just go home. This vacation can't end soon enough."

He ignored her. The exit was a mile away.

Once they pulled off the highway, John could see that Cammy oversold the Southern-ness of the town: it was overrun by shops aimed at the psychic tourist. Or maybe Cammy went so long ago that the town had changed. John really had no idea how old she was or, for that matter, how many boyfriends she'd had. He was just sure she was single now.

"Where do you want to go?" he asked.

"John, I don't care."

"Let's go there," he said, pointing at a shop. The front was open to the street. T-shirts hung out front. There was a sorry paper mâché statue of what was probably supposed to be one of the Cassadaga Children. John thought it was scary because it was so terrible, like that obscene Lucille Ball statue he'd seen in Suzie's hometown during last year's vacation. She'd been bored then, as well, but he thought it was funny.

He parked the car. Susan didn't even look when he got out. She just leaned the seat back and closed her eyes. He walked inside. A ceiling fan turned lazily overhead. The shade in the store was nice and kept it cool. He started to look around. He wanted to get something for Cammy, for when he saw her again. Just to let her know he'd been thinking about her. But it couldn't be too big. It needed to be something that he could hide, but pass off as nothing if he were caught. So no "Cassadaga, wish you were here" pencils, no keychains with hearts, no cards with dirty limericks. He fumbled around with the knick-knacks until he found it: a Cassadaga churchkey. What better thing to get a waitress at a bar than a bottle opener? And what better way to show her he'd been thinking about her than to go to the place she mentioned to get it?

He paid $11.95 to the bored clerk. He waved off the proffered bag and receipt and dropped the churchkey into the pocket of his swim trunks, next to his car keys.

He stepped back into the sunlight. Susan was outside the car now, leaning against it, eyes closed, sunning herself. John thought that Susan looked pretty— above average with nice tits. But she wasn't as alluring as Cammy. A five minute conversation kept Cammy on his mind. Susan could never pull that off.

She heard his steps and opened her eyes. "I've changed my mind," she said.

"Oh?"

"I want to go there," she said, pointing at a sign that read: '*Intuitive Energy Spiritual Healer.*' "I think it could be fun."

They walked inside and into a wall of incense smoke. John's eyes watered as he tried to adjust to the low light. They walked past purple wall hangings and ancient easy chairs, through a wall of hanging beads, and into a room with cushions on the floor surrounding a round table. An older woman sat at the table. She had tanned too much in her youth and was paying for it now. Her hair, black streaked with silver, was pulled back and covered by a colorful silk handkerchief. She wore a billowing kimono. John didn't think she looked like a psychic.

"You'd like a healing?" she asked.

"The two of us," Susan said. "Do you do couples?"

"Of course," the woman said. "For the two of you it will be $100."

Susan fished into her purse, counted out the bills, and handed them to the healer.

"Please," she said. "Sit."

They settled in next to one another.

The woman looked at them and scowled. "Hands on the table," she said. Susan looked at John, reached out. The woman eyed him as he, reluctant, turned his hand palm up and Susan rested her hand in his.

The woman closed her eyes and rocked back. "It's easy to see," she said. She pointed at John. "You aren't happy."

Susan nodded. "We've been fighting," she admitted.

The woman pointed at John. "People come between you two. And you let them."

John saw Susan nodding out of the corner of his eye. He looked away. The woman leaned forward. "There's more than one person between you two."

John stood up and turned to leave. He slipped on a cushion and sprawled on the floor. Susan rushed to help him, but he pushed her back and stormed out of the place. He knew what kind of woman the fortune teller was: she would support another member of the *sisterhood* no matter what. He would never get a fair shake with a bitch like that.

Susan caught up with him outside as he stomped to the car. He glanced over his shoulder at her. "You told her to say that!"

"How?" Susan asked, trailing behind him. "When would I do that?"

"When I was in that shop!" he said.

"John," she said. "That was for, like, two minutes. I didn't have time."

They reached the car. He glowered at her.

"What did you get in there, anyway?" she asked.

"Let's go." He hit a button on the car's remote. The doors unlocked with a thud.

They made it back on the highway before Susan spoke up again. "Do you want to tell me what that was about?"

"Since we left the bar— " he paused, getting his story straight, "—since we left the bar you've done nothing but accuse me of cheating on you. I think you're redirecting. You're disappointed Tim didn't show."

"John, Tim is my friend. That's it. You need to stop," She went on: "And something was up with that waitress."

"Cammy," he said.

Susan couldn't help herself. "How sweet of you to remember."

John had to take a deep breath to relax. God, how he wished he could hit her. "She's not a threat to you, Susan. You were right: she probably was flirting to get a better tip. I just don't think she was expecting you to be the one to pay."

"Tell me why you wouldn't want her instead of me," Susan said.

John shook his head. "She's so trashy, Susan. She's— she's so white trash."

"That's a start," Susan said. "Go on."

"Look, Susan, she's just so far below me."

John looked over at her. He could tell something wasn't sitting right.

"None of those things have to do with me, John," she said.

He shook his head, stared straight ahead. "It doesn't matter what I say."

He heard her take a deep breath, let it out. "I'm sorry," she said, "I'm being too hard on you. Let's just relax, not talk for a while. We'll get home, have a small, quiet dinner, and sleep on things."

He glanced over at her. She looked pleasant, relaxed.

Susan unbuckled her seatbelt and was out of the car before John had taken his keys out of the ignition. She stretched, smiling, happy to be home. She bent down and looked into the car at John, who still sat in the driver's seat. He looked bemused.

"John," she said, walking to the back of the car, "can you open the trunk?"

She started wrenching her suitcase out of the back. John joined her and helped her pull it out before reaching for his bag.

"John, can you give me your keys?"

He let go of his bag and straightened up. "Where are yours?"

"I can't find them."

He turned back to his bag. "Can you just wait a minute?"

"You have more than one bag, you'll have your hands full." He handed his keys over. "Thank you, honey."

She took them and dragged her bag up the stairs as quickly as she could. When she'd reached the door he was at the bottom of their stairs. Moving fast, she unlocked the door, pushed her bag in ahead of her, and slammed the door behind her. She threw the deadbolt: even if he somehow had another set of keys he couldn't get inside.

Susan relaxed. John banged on the door, yelling her name, but even with just a door between them she felt better.

The banging stopped and she could hear John stomp down the stairs.

"Suzie!"

She stepped onto the balcony and watched him. She got her phone out and pointed it at him. She pulled up the camera, turned it to video, and hit record. "I'm dumping you, John. You're an asshole. Something in you snapped today."

He stared at her. Rooted. Then: "You *bitch!* I was supposed to be dumping you!"

He looked around and, only finding pebbles on the asphalt, grabbed those and hurled them at her. She just watched as they splashed the wall around her. She kept her phone trained on him. "You're a fucking whore!" he bellowed. She said nothing. He started kicking her car. He stopped, winded.

Then he pulled a churchkey out of his pocket. He put it against her car and dragged it through the paint, leaving a deep gouge. He screamed at her all the while.

A voice from the adjoining balcony: "What's going on?"

Suzie looked over and smiled at an elderly man she only thought of as 1095-C. "I dumped him," she said.

"He's not handling it well."

John threw the churchkey at her. "Not at all," she said.

1095-C looked between the two, then fixated on Susan. "Should I call the police?"

Susan kept her phone trained on John. "Yes, please. I need to keep gathering evidence."

"I'm sorry, Suzie." John looked scared. "Don't call the police."

She looked over at 1095-C. "Don't worry," he said, "I'm dialing."

"You want to go back to Cammy, John?"

He looked shocked. She could hear 1095-C talking.

John broke down into screams and yells. When the police arrived a few minutes later he was still at it. He didn't help himself when he punched the responding officer who was trying to defuse the situation.

An hour later, John was gone, a report was filed, and it was just Susan and 1095-C at their balconies. "Do you need anything?" he asked her.

"Thank you," she said, "but I'm okay."

"Breakups are hard, but he'll make it harder."

"It's okay," she said, finding a number on her phone. "I know a guy who might be better for me, if only he'd answer the phone."

—

John W. Treviño still doesn't know how he got here: nothing in his life prepared him to be a writer. He works in insurance regulation, praying that no one figures out his middle name; he once accidentally lit a workplace on fire by misusing a toaster; and he studied English murderers and their executions in school.

The Wall

By Anna Leah Karasik

116

It blinks.

It blinks.

The cursor taps its toe.
    It mocks my futile
    Quest to create.

I think.

I think.

The page is blank.
    Depressing. White. I
    Must shut my eyes.

I blink.

Ideas buzz about
    Splatting into The Wall.
    Bugs on a windshield,
    Oozing creative juices—
    Stains—reminders
    Of the thoughts
    I almost

I sink.

I sink to the floor in a gracious bow
    Out of respect for his highness, The Prince.
    The Prince of The Wall, tall and dark, knew how
    To block off brilliant thoughts, to bravely fence
    Against the mightiest creative minds.

I drink.

I drink.

My eyelids are heavy with dark liquor,
    The Prince is pouring out more. I ask him,
    "What tactics did Shakespeare use to conquer
    This fortress?"

He laughs. "Shakespeare did not win
    His battle against The Wall. No man can."

I hang my head, but The Prince lifts my chin.
    He refills the goblet and says, "no *man*."

The Prince, he winks.

My cheeks turn pink.

I blink.

Who winked?

Drool.
    I fell asleep
    By the white screen.

The cursor blinks.

I think.

Shakespeare winks.

I nod to The Bard, I know what to do.
　　I smile and say, "Then, I'll charm The Prince, too."

I type,
　　"It blinks."

Beyond the Relic

By JD Pagano

Isaam stroked Moosha under his chin, making the camel grunt in approval and lap at Isaam's face with his coarse tongue. The sun rose high over the desert, and Moosha's soft, curly mane glistened under its rays. Tan sand swirled in the gentle breeze around them, and Isaam wiped the camel's slobber from his face, lest wind-blown grit stick to it.

Despite the heat that day, Isaam hardly minded. For he was djinn, a creature born out of the sands. To his cool blue skin, the golden glow of the sun felt like a mother's embrace, soothing.

Isaam took a soft-bristled brush and combed Moosha's coat, one long stroke after another. Each pass tugged at knots in the camel's fur or loosened clumps of sand. He started just behind the ear and worked his way toward the rear. Once one side was complete, he switched to the other and repeated. It was a slow and steady process, but one performed in peaceful silence. As Isaam worked, his mind emptied, his racing thoughts and worries fading away. For a brief window in the day, nothing else mattered. It was just Isaam, Moosha, and the brush.

That was, until Moosha interrupted his serenity. "You missed a spot," the camel said dryly.

Isaam squinted, eyeing the camel's curly fur. "I did *not*."

"And be sure to brush my mane over to the right," Moosha continued. "That way it frames my good side."

"You're a camel. You don't have a good side."

Moosha flared his nostrils and snorted. "I do! Everyone knows my eyelashes are thicker on the left."

Isaam grumbled under his breath but relented, combing the camel's mane as requested. Even after all these years, Isaam still wasn't used to

Moosha talking. It was his djinn wish-granting magic that had made it so. Many droughts ago, the master had been drunk off his ass on wine—as humans so often were. Bored, he'd wished for the camel to speak, thinking it would prove entertaining.

Moosha shifted one hip after the other, twitching his booty in a way designed to draw attention. "You missed another spot."

"You already made that joke," Isaam sighed. Entertaining, indeed. "Who are you trying to look pretty for, anyway?"

"Master Saeed's business partners are sure to ride up on camels. Some of them might be cute. You never know," the camel said.

"Djinn, hurry with the beast," Beaker yelled from across the camp. "They'll be here shortly." The man pulled back his once-white turban and wiped the sweat from his brow. He wore an emerald green kaftan that hung to his ankles, decorated with intricately embroidered red roses. The robe was far too heavy for this time of year, but Beaker wore it, anyway. It was his finest, and Isaam assumed his master—not too unlike Moosha—wore it to impress whomever might arrive soon. "And don't give him more water. The bastard bit me earlier."

His back was to Isaam when he snapped his fingers. "And fetch me more wine." He didn't wait for a response before returning to his brown wool tent.

Beaker was human, or "thin-skin," as Isaam preferred to call them. He was not a terrible master, all things considered. After 300 years of granting wishes to various men, Isaam had certainly seen worse. Beaker, like so many masters before, could not be bothered to use Isaam's name. So, Isaam offered the man mutual respect—which was to say, he only referred to him by his long, hawk-like nose.

"Yes, master," Isaam replied in a level tone. He pulled the basin of water away from the camel.

If Beaker was merely rude to Isaam, he might have let it slide. After all, as a servant, Isaam expected little. But the human was rude to the camels, too, and Isaam couldn't tolerate that.

Moosha bared his teeth in a gummy smile, then drooped his head and batted a pretty, twinkling eye at Isaam. The djinn was forced to look away. What kind of heartless thin-skin would be cruel to such a cute, fluffy camel?

"Oh come, now," Isaam said with a laugh. "You got extra just this morning!"

The camel nuzzled his fuzzy fur against Isaam's chest. The djinn rolled his eyes. "*Fine.*" He pushed the basin of water back into reach.

"See? That's why I stay pretty." Moosha winked at the djinn before craning his neck down to lap up more water.

After giving Moosha one last pat on the head, Isaam pulled the water basin away, for good this time. Next, he scurried over to the wagon and crouched beside the leather supply packs. There, he fumbled for a vintage of wine that Beaker might like. A twenty-year-old red from the east? No. Perhaps with the heat, a white might be in order. It was always hard to guess the whims of Beaker.

Before Isaam could decide, the distant neigh of horses drew his attention. They crested the nearest dune, a party of four figures clad in identical, loose black robes and burgundy turbans. Two of them rode alone, while the other two pulled a horse-drawn cart. In the back of the cart lay a large wrought-iron cage, and, within it, an enormous, winged beast.

Isaam had found it rather odd that they should trek so far into the desert to conduct business. What was the master up to that required such secrecy? But now, seeing the cage, he knew. The trade of wild creatures was highly illegal in Zagormesh.

But that was the way with Beaker. After gaining a wish-granting djinn, wealth beyond imagine, and even a talking camel, the human had grown bored and now apparently turned to the illegal procurement of rare beasts to keep himself occupied. The realization soured Isaam's mood, and he scowled.

Beaker emerged from his tent, still fidgeting with the ruby-embedded brooch he'd pinned to his turban. While the figures approached, Beaker continued to brush the sand from his kaftan and fiddle with the sapphire ring that adorned his finger.

"Peace upon you, Faraj," Beaker said with a boisterous voice as the figures dismounted from their horses. He had a slick smile on his face, and his arms were spread out wide.

Though their faces were veiled, Isaam could see the smoke swirling from their breath and the weathered red skin around their sharp, crimson eyes. Ifrits.

The ifrit in front lowered his veil. "Saeed," Faraj said, drawing out the *s* like a snake and skipping the customary greeting. He pulled a scimitar from its sheath, the metal scraping as it came free. As he brandished the weapon, the polished blade scintillated under the bright sun.

"Come now, bringing a weapon to a negotiation? How uncouth," Beaker said.

The ifrit coughed out a laugh and ran a finger along the smooth blade. "Negotiations with your kind usually require them."

Isaam made a small nod of agreement. He supposed that even ifrits—another kind of djinn—disliked their sworn servitude.

Beaker scoffed but said no more. Apparently, the old man was wise enough to not argue with ifrits who had short tempers and long blades.

"Do you have what we've come for?" Faraj asked.

"Of course, of course," said Beaker, as he snapped his fingers. "Djinn, fetch the chest."

Even after so many years, being called in that way made Isaam shudder. How he longed for a day free of service to humans. But it was a foolish notion. Like all djinn, he was duty bound by Solomon's curse: doomed to spend his days granting *their* wishes.

Isaam turned his attention to a large wooden chest that sat beside the wine packs. He clasped it in both hands and heaved with all his might. But the chest didn't budge. Whatever treasure lay within was far too heavy for him.

"Pardon, master, would you be so kind as to assist?" Isaam asked.

"Fine," Beaker growled. "I *wish* you would bring me the chest. And be quick about it."

At first, nothing happened. They all stood there in anticipatory silence.

There was a flash, and for a moment, white light blinded Isaam. His body tingled, surging with a familiar energy as the wish's magic took form. His muscles popped and groaned as they swelled. One long, engorged vein made itself known down his left bicep. Suddenly, the djinn was twice the size he'd been only a moment before.

This time, he lifted the chest with ease, as though it were a toy in his muscled arms. As he carried it from the wagon to Beaker, he grinned. There was not a lot of glamor in being a Solomon-cursed djinn, the highlight being the inventive ways he found to grant the wishes.

After reaching the gathering, Isaam dropped the chest next to his master, the wood thudding as it pressed into the soft sand. He bowed. "As you command," he said in a terribly deep, rumbling voice.

The light flashed again and a whistling sound emanated, like air leaked from a waterskin. Isaam's body folded into itself, his muscles withering as they returned to their normal size.

Just then, the sunlight caught the flat of Faraj's scimitar, and Isaam found the sharp blade too close to his decidedly fleshy, unprotected blue skin. With a skip in his step, he retreated to the cage, well away from any mortal peril. There, he inspected the captive creature. It was a roc, easily thrice his size. Red and brown feathers covered its back, though patches were missing, bald pink skin exposed. The feathers faded to white near the creature's golden, hooked beak and sharp talons. The roc crouched awkwardly within the cage, unable to spread its wings in the confined space.

Isaam imagined it soaring among the clouds, free as he wished himself to be. "Don't worry, my friend," he whispered, wrapping his fingers around the iron bars. "I will free you somehow, someday."

"Your payment," Beaker announced, tapping the lid of the heavy chest.

The ifrits stared at it with eager eyes. Beaker took a long-stemmed brass key from his pocket and slid it into the chest's iron lock, twisting until it made a satisfying *clack*. With a cocky grin, Beaker ripped back the lid.

The air above the chest gleamed from the reflected light. There was a brief pause as their collective eyes adjusted. And then, all at once, they took a step toward the chest, drawn in by the treasure.

After Isaam saw the gold medallions that were held within, his brow creased in awe. All his life, he'd been surrounded by greedy masters and material wealth, but even he was impressed at the sight. Even with the help of Isaam's wishes, it still would have taken Beaker years to collect that much gold.

Faraj approached the chest first and shoved the pointy end of his blade into the pool of precious metal. Using the scimitar, he dragged the medallions aside to take a deeper look. It was gold all the way down.

Faraj cackled. "You're short." The other four ifrits unsheathed their blades.

The air suddenly felt thicker, hotter.

Isaam had no notion of what a captured roc might cost, but he couldn't imagine anything costing more than the contents of the chest before them.

"Short!" Beaker cried, flinging his hands into the air. "This much gold should garner three of the beasts!"

"What can I say," Faraj said, brushing sand from his shoulder. "Our master says this isn't enough." The ifrit took a step closer to Beaker.

Isaam nervously adjusted the turban he wore over his coarse, black hair. He hardly cared for Beaker, but still, he had no interest in seeing the man harmed.

Beaker held his palms up. "Okay, okay. I'm a reasonable man. You want more? Very well, then. I just need more time." Fat drops of sweat rolled down his flushed cheeks. He took a step back, shying away from Faraj. "A few more months, and I can get more gold. Yes, I'm quite certain of it."

"Oh, I think you have plenty of value to barter with," Faraj said, a sly smile creeping across his face. The ifrit extended the scimitar toward Beaker and clanked the end against the man's sapphire ring, the large gem within it glowing with soft blue light. "My master will take the djinn as payment, then." His voice was calm, as though the conclusion were obvious.

"What? No, absolutely not," Beaker said. "The djinn is priceless. He's worth far more than this creature."

"Is that so?" Faraj said as he dragged his blade through the sands. "A shame then, that you were short." The ifrit clicked his tongue.

But his disappointment seemed forced, and Isaam didn't quite believe the act. Had these ifrits ever wanted the gold? Was it all a ploy to lure Beaker into the desert? All to steal Isaam and his wishes?

"Please, please! Be reasonable. What else can I give you? We have wine. Wine!" Beaker said. He fell backward to the ground.

Faraj advanced, stalking his prey. He loomed tall, casting the old man in shadows. He drew his scimitar high overhead.

"No!" Isaam cried.

But he was too late.

Isaam flinched, averting his gaze, unable to witness the act. Unable to watch harm befall his master—even after the years of poor treatment Isaam had suffered at his hands. Still, he heard the blade slice through the fine emerald cloth of Beaker's kaftan and the cry of pain that followed.

Then the ifrits grabbed the old man, wrenching the ring from his finger. The sapphire pulsed one last time before disappearing beneath Faraj's cloak.

"Well now, what's fair is fair," Faraj called, as one of the other ifrits unlatched the horses from the cart that held the roc's cage. "The beast would only slow us down." Faraj swung his leg over his horse. "When our master adorns your relic," he shouted to Isaam, "she will summon you to her side." He cracked a whip, the horses neighed, and the ifrits were off. They galloped up the same dune they'd come from, crested its hill, and vanished off into the vast desert beyond.

For a passing moment, Isaam stood there, nonplussed. Dark thoughts bubbled at the edge of his consciousness. What if he didn't help? What if he let Beaker die? But he quickly pushed the terrible notion from his mind. He would not be a monster. He would not be like *them*.

Forcing himself out of his own stupor, Isaam rushed to his master's side and cradled the old man in his arms. Even holding him, Isaam dared not look down; he'd never been good with the sight of blood.

"Say it. Say the words," Isaam pleaded. "Wish for your wound to be healed."

"I wish..." the man began, dragging out each syllable, his voice thin.

"I can't help until you say it."

"...my wound..." Beaker continued, but his eyes were glassy, barely able to remain open. Isaam heard him scrabbling at his tunic, feeling for the small, hard lump beneath it. Daring a glance down, Isaam saw that there was a sudden awareness in his master's eyes. The old man opened his mouth as if to speak.

But no words came.

His eyes closed. His hand fell away limp.

And then Isaam felt it, the sudden change, as though a weight was lifted from his chest. He blinked, and blinked again, hardly able to believe it had happened. Hardly able to process what had come to pass.

A torrent of conflicting emotions raged within Isaam, battling for control. He had loathed Beaker, despised that he was rude and lazy and, worst of all, *human*. But he was still a person, a creature of God. Maybe Beaker—no, Saeed—hadn't been a kind master, but he didn't deserve to die like this.

Drawn on by instinct, Isaam lifted Saeed's head and removed the chain, revealing the brass pendant that had hung around his neck religiously for the last forty years. Isaam's relic.

Over the years, many who coveted a wish-granting djinn for themselves had attempted to steal Isaam's relic from Saeed. Recently, the man had taken to wearing the sapphire ring as a decoy relic. Faraj's master would be in for quite a surprise when she adorned the ring, tried to summon Isaam, and absolutely nothing happened.

Hidden away under his master's kaftan, Isaam had hardly seen his own relic in years. A bluish patina now blemished its brassy veneer. He pressed the thin medallion between his fingers, massaging its rough surface, and exhaled a long breath—as though he could breathe deeply for the very first time in his whole life.

At long last, after three centuries of service, Isaam was free.

He'd daydreamed about this moment. He had imagined it a million ways: a glorious scimitar battle, a daring gamble in a game of cards, a clever ruse to trick the late master. But no matter how it started, it always ended the same way, with Isaam dancing and shouting from the rooftops, bursting with joy.

But much to the djinn's surprise, he felt nothing like that just then. Though he wasn't hungry, a terrible ache gnawed at his stomach. Relic in hand, he crossed his arms over his belly and hunched forward, until his forehead rested against his late master's blood-soaked chest.

Isaam kneeled in the sands beside Saeed for some time, too stunned to move, with only the whistling winds to interrupt the lonely silence.

Eventually, a squawk drew Isaam from his daze. Only then did he remember the roc, still trapped inside its cage. Minutes earlier, the magnificent bird had been of great value, at the center of their transaction. Now it was ignored, completely abandoned in favor of greater treasure. Isaam spat to the side, disgusted.

He rose and, though he felt numb and his legs were wobbly, he willed himself over to the cage. The roc squawked and writhed against the iron-wrought bars of its prison.

"Hey, there," he said, his voice soothing. "It's okay. I'm going to get you out of there." Isaam took the cage's metal lock in his hand. "I wish I had the key to this lock," he said. But he knew the wish was useless. For he had no master now, no means of harnessing his magic.

He'd just have to do it the old-fashioned way.

Isaam scanned the camp, looking for anything that might be useful. There was no crowbar. No sword. Nothing obvious he could use for leverage. Then he remembered constructing Master Saeed's tent just the night before. He went to it and wrenched loose one of the steel rods that comprised its frame. Returning to the roc's cage, he wedged the steel rod between the door and lock, and hoisted with all his might. "I wish I still had my strength from earlier," he said sardonically.

He tried and tried to no avail; either the lock was too strong or he was too weak. He switched to swinging the rod. A lot of clanks and curses later, and still the lock remained intact. Each blow had rattled the cage. The great bird shifted wildly within, alarmed by the violence.

"Argh!" Isaam cried and threw the rod into the sands. "I can't help you. I'm useless without my magic." His shoulders sagged.

The roc cocked its head to the side, big wet eyes looking on at Isaam.

Isaam imagined how the ifrits had treated the roc. He wondered how long it had been caged, how long its masters had prevented it from soaring among the winds, as God intended for it. When was its last meal? Where was its family?

No, Isaam would not let this creature suffer any longer.

With teeth clenched, Isaam grabbed the steel rod once more. He wedged it between the cage and lock, holding it so tight his knuckles turned white. He heaved with all his might, heaved with all the pent up anger he felt at Master Saeed, at the ifrits.

There was a ripping sound. The lock fell into the sands. The cage door swung open.

Isaam took a few steps back, giving the roc a wide berth. The cage was so small compared to the enormous creature that it shuffled out awkwardly. Its talons sunk into the soft sand, and it stretched its wings wide.

Isaam blinked at the beast in awe. Spread out, its wings were massive, perhaps fifty strides in total. This close, the feathers were more nuanced and multicolored: scarlet that faded to crimson and on to burgundy. Had he ever seen such a magnificent creature?

Then, the roc cooed, in a way that Isaam hoped might be appreciation.

"You're welcome," Isaam said with a faint smile.

The roc flapped its wings and shot into the air. A dust cloud swirled in its wake. Isaam covered his mouth with his sleeve to keep from coughing.

As the Roc sailed high into the sky, it turned back to Isaam and chirped once more.

Isaam waved. "Goodbye, friend."

After the roc disappeared into the distance, Isaam walked over to the caravan, to his oldest friend.

"Brother." Isaam ran his fingers through the camel's mane.

"Brother," Moosha replied. For once, his voice was quiet, having caught wind of Isaam's solemn mood. "You are free now. A celebration seems in order."

"I guess I am," Isaam said, at nearly a whisper. "But a man just died. Celebration does not feel right."

Though he wasn't eating, Moosha chewed on the air, in a way Isaam knew as the camel's means of shrugging. "What will you do next, then?"

Isaam didn't answer. Instead, he kept running his hands through the camel's fur, processing the ordeal. They stood there like that for some time, just the two of them in the vast, lonely desert. Even though Isaam was centuries old, he had no idea what came next. He had spent so many years wishing to be free, yet he never thought what he might do, should it ever come to pass.

Finally, he leaned forward until their foreheads touched, and he smiled. It was a small, thin smile, but it was honest and came from his heart.

"Brother, I don't know what comes next," Isaam said. "But let's find out together."

—

JD Pagano doesn't like talking about himself; that's why he prefers the company of his two cats, who rarely ask him personal questions. He works in healthcare technology, where, during the endless barrage of meetings, he daydreams about fantasy worlds. His loving wife, Amanda, made him write some of those ideas down.

Editor & Illustrator Bios

Shina Shayesteh is an editor, writer, artist, lover of history, longtime member of Onwards, and is purportedly at least 3% Eldritch abomination. She volunteered to edit this anthology because she thought it would be more palatable to stay in the shadows and nitpick everyone else's work than to have to submit her own and suffer the pressure of being seen and known (eugh!). When she's not being a menace to her beloved friends, she serves as Editor-in-Chief for the national non-profit organization Strong Towns.

—

Derek Hsu is the cover art illustrator. He often draws at the writing meetups not because he's trying to be special, but because he's an inspired manga artist. The only thing he loves more than talking about his manga idea is karaoke.